KNIGHT'S ARDOR

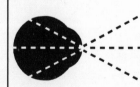

This Large Print Book carries the
Seal of Approval of N.A.V.H.

Knight's Ardor

Teresa Swift

THORNDIKE PRESS
A part of Gale, Cengage Learning

GALE
CENGAGE Learning

Detroit • New York • San Francisco • New Haven, Conn • Waterville, Maine • London

GALE
CENGAGE Learning

LIBRARY OF CONGRESS CATALOGING-IN-PUBLICATION DATA

Swift, Teresa.
   Knight's ardor / by Teresa Swift.
      p. cm. — (Thorndike Press large print gentle romance)
   ISBN-13: 978-1-4104-4226-0 (hardcover)
   ISBN-10: 1-4104-4226-8 (hardcover) 1. Ladies-in-waiting—Fiction.
  2. Nobility—England—Fiction. 3. Knights and knighthood—England—Fiction. 4. England—Social life and customs—1066–1485—Fiction.
  5. Large type books. I. Title.
  PR6119.W547K58 2011b
  823'.92—dc22   2011032080

Published in 2011 by arrangement with Thomas Bouregy & Co., Inc.

For Daniel, who kept telling me to write a book

PROLOGUE

You deceived me, Alexander Ringewar, Rosamund thought angrily. *I could have borne it if your duty had taken you away. I could have borne it if you had never shown the slightest interest in me.* But he had kissed her, their arms wrapped around each other like the tangle of forest branches and creeper that had surrounded them. He had whispered her name like it had meant something to him. Now he danced in another woman's arms. The wind atop the battlements whipped Rosamund's hair, and she brushed it away from her face furiously. Tears pricked at her eyelids. *No,* she thought. *I have not cried for you before; I will not cry now.* She had indulged in a foolish fantasy, and tonight was nothing but the bleakest of reminders.

CHAPTER ONE

Five months earlier

One moment Rosamund was riding; the next, she was falling. As she hit the ground, the breath was slammed from her chest and pain jolted through her. Stunned though she was, her overwhelming instinct was to get up fast and get away. But it was too late. Even as she rolled over to rise, she felt an iron grip upon her. The weight of another human body pinned her to the leaf-strewn ground. She struggled, but it was no use against her assailant's superior strength. Then, as her hood fell back from her head, his grip suddenly eased. She heard surprise in his voice.

"A woman!"

She seized the opportunity to wrest her arms free, but her advantage was only momentary. She quickly found herself held fast again.

"Let me go!" Fear and anger swirled in

equal measure within her as she wrestled in vain against her captor. Her panic mounted as he started to move a hand over her body. Then she realized he was searching for weapons. He would find she had none.

"Who are you? What's your business out here?" he asked as he concluded his search. His voice was hard but well spoken.

"I live in these parts," Rosamund gasped. "I ride out where I choose; it's no concern of yours." She gritted her teeth as she struggled again. "I say again, let me go."

"You live on the manor? You take an innocent ride, nothing more?" The man's voice was a fraction more measured, but his grip remained unchanged. Above her, his face was shadowy in the dimness of the wood's early morning.

"Yes, and who are you to ask? You have no cause to waylay me in such a fashion. Release me."

He did not accede to her demand but studied her face for a moment.

"On the contrary, I have cause enough. I would take you for an outlaw, skulking in the forest at such an hour and dressed so." He took a swift glance down at her male clothing and dark cloak. "You speak well, yet you dress like no nobleman's wife or daughter I have ever seen. But I have known of women turned outlaw, though they haven't lived long. Who are you? How would you assure me of your intentions? I have little patience for thieves or worse."

In her outrage at his accusation, she was about to speak her name, but then she stopped. There was a fine ransom to be had for the release of a nobleman — or woman — held hostage. Perhaps it would be better not to reveal her identity to her captor if she could help it.

"My intentions?" she snapped despite her fear. "I might ask you the same. You are the stranger here, not I. You see I carry no weapon. I cannot hurt you, but you are hurting me," she finished, pushing against the arms holding her hard against the ground, to emphasize her point.

"If I let you go, do you promise me you will not run?"

"I promise you nothing."

"Then I shall not release you, but bind you, and appropriate your horse, and let the next village's authorities deal with you." He flicked his eyes toward their two horses, his own close by, hers a few yards away; both were well schooled enough to remain near their riders. "Which is it to be?"

Outrage battled with pragmatism before she muttered her grudging reply.

"Very well. I shan't run."

The stranger carefully let go of her, kneeling back, then rising, his eyes fixed unwaveringly upon her.

Rosamund got to her feet and backed away a pace. As she did so, she staggered a little, a stab of pain shooting up her side.

"Are you injured?" the man asked.

She shook her head. She had fallen heavily, but not awkwardly, and she had landed on the wood's carpet of leafy detritus, thankfully avoiding contact with the unforgiving solidity of a tree trunk. Despite her fear, she was annoyed about the fall: had her horse not stumbled and lurched, she would never have lost her balance so. As it was, it did not feel like too serious an injury. Bruised, most likely a day or two's discomfort. She had suffered worse. She was far more relieved that this man seemingly had no wish to force himself upon her nor rob her, these being her initial fears when he had caught sight of her and pursued her. So far, he seemed more concerned with her intentions than in acting upon any malign purpose of his own. He would surely not have inquired after her well-being if he himself intended to harm her, nor would he have agreed to let her go. But she was still angry and fearful.

"You have still not told me who you are," the man said.

"And neither, sir, have you," Rosamund retorted.

He narrowed shrewd eyes at her, considering her rejoinder.

"My name is Alexander Ringewar, a knight loyal to the king. My business remains my own for now. Suffice to say I act only to protect myself on my legitimate travels through these parts."

"Then our intentions are one and the same," said Rosamund sharply.

With the benefit of the greater distance now between them, she took in the man's appearance for the first time. He stood at least six feet tall, which was taller than most of the men Rosamund knew. He was broadly built, though not stocky, and had the browned face of a man who spent much of his time outdoors. Now that she had time to recognize it, she could see he wore the apparel of a knight of considerable rank. His short mail hauberk, worn for riding rather than battle, was covered with a gold-fringed blue surcoat upon which the symbol of a gold-and-white eagle stretched its wings. Strong, masculine features lent him a natural authority; his hair was a dark blond in the forest's early light. With senses instinctively attuned to every nuance of the situation, Rosamund tried to interpret his expression. His face had a seriousness to it, no hint of humor. Rosamund had no doubt it was the face of someone who had seen much to sober the soul in what she guessed to be a good thirty years. But there was no obvious leer of malice in his countenance. His brow was furrowed in concentration.

"Your husband allows you to ride unaccompanied through the woods in times like these?"

If Alexander Ringewar were skeptical of her guarded protestations, she could hardly blame him. She had no such permission. Rosamund avoided answering his question, unwilling to be cowed into obedient response.

"I have no husband."

"Your father, then?"

Rosamund stonewalled. "It is my own business where and when I ride, but I am anything but an outlaw, I can assure you of that. You found for yourself I have no weapons, and I am no threat to you." She busied herself with brushing her clothes of the dirt that clung to them from her fall.

As he continued to frown at her, she guessed that, just as she had done, he was assessing her age, noting the quality of her

14

speech, and judging her rank and position accordingly. Despite her uninformative answer, he seemed to relax a little.

"It's business of mine when I hear somebody shadowing me in a forest."

"Shadowing you? I do not shadow you," Rosamund protested. "It is entirely the opposite! The first I knew of you was the knowledge that you sought to follow me, not I you. When I saw you riding at me, naturally I was frightened and fled." She scowled. "And I can't think why I offer you an explanation when it is you who has chased me and held me against my will." Unconsciously, she rubbed her arms where he had gripped her, the memory of his terrifying closeness still vivid.

He gave her a searching look. "If you are to be believed, then you have my apologies if I have hurt you. I mean you no harm, but these are uncertain times. A traveler cannot be too careful. Even a woman as —" he hesitated. "Even a woman might not be all she seems." He studied her again. "I'm none the wiser of your purpose here, but let me make one thing plain: the woods close to the road are not a safe place for a woman on her own, no matter who she is. Robbers are known to target such places for easy pickings from travelers. If you are here in all innocence, I urge you to take better caution."

"I have frequented these woods all my life," snapped Rosamund, "and have come across none who have hurt me, save you."

Alexander was stopped from replying by the faint sound of two long horn blows. A reconnaissance requested. *He must be with a party,* thought Rosamund. They both turned their heads toward the sound. Alexander broke off his attention to Rosamund and strode toward his horse.

Rosamund hesitated. She had promised not to run, and yet this was her chance. Was it wrong to break a promise to a man who had scared the very life out of her? She gave a low whistle to her horse. Alexander Ringewar halted and turned. Rosamund's horse trotted over and stood nudging her. She caught up his reins. If it came to another mounted chase, they would have an even start, both within a step of mounting their horses. If Alexander ran back toward her, Rosamund calculated, she ought to have just enough time to mount and flee before he reached her. Yet to abscond now would make her look guilty just when he seemed convinced of the opposite.

"I will not run," Rosamund declared, anticipating his thoughts as he stared at her, his eyes hard. "I gave my word. And as I hold to that promise, I would have you believe all else I say. In my turn, I believe you also, that you mean me no harm, and I trust that, since neither of us has any unworthy business with the other, you will allow me to leave unhindered."

In the silence after her words, the distant horn sounded twice again. Alexander seemed to make up his mind. He pulled his own horn from a saddlebag and put it to his lips; a single long note of reassurance issued. As his reply sounded, Rosamund moved to mount her horse, ignoring the pain in her side as she did so. Seated astride once again, she gathered up her reins and waited for him to reply. When he did, he surprised her.

"If you are merely an early rider in these parts, then perhaps I ought offer to accompany you home," Alexander mused, his steady gaze upon her again.

Rosamund couldn't help but laugh bitterly.

"First you attack and unseat me, and now you offer me an escort?" Or perhaps, she thought, it was a further attempt to ascertain more about her.

"You must understand why I acted as I did," Alexander replied. "But I would not neglect my duty to an honest fellow traveler."

"You owe no duty to me, sir," said Rosamund curtly. "If you have no objection, I give you my leave." She turned abruptly and began to weave away through the trees. This time, Alexander Ringewar did not pursue her.

Alexander had already decided to let Rosamund go. Patrolling the route ahead for his fellow soldiers, he had jumped to the alert when he had caught sight of the dark-cloaked rider through the trees. His suspicions had been heightened when the other figure became aware of him and drifted quickly away. He was seasoned at forest tracking; it did not take him long to refind his quarry. Aware of being followed, the cloaked figure had made a break for the open road. It was only poor luck that his horse had stumbled as Alexander gained upon him, allowing Alexander the chance to unseat him with an outstretched arm. Except that the "he" had turned out to be a "she." A well-spoken, extremely attractive she, at that. One sentence from her mouth established that she was a young woman of rank rather than the peasantry; the smoothness of her hands confirmed it. The obedience of her steed also indicated a connection to a noble's stableyard. Why she was dressed in the hose and shirt of a man was as yet beyond him, but, at that point, Alexander's initial suspicions of having encountered a ne'er-do-well were dissipating. Her lack of weaponry further supported the conclusion that she was harmless, but he had thought it as well to investigate a little further, for the encounter was an unlikely one for the very reasons he had proceeded to outline to her.

Alexander doubted that any male overseer of hers was aware of her presence in the forest. He suspected she wanted to keep it that way. While it was never wise to antagonize a captor, her spirited refusal to talk was notable, for she must have been scared. Her discretion might also have been born of a more subtle intelligence: ill advised though she was to be traversing the forest on her own, she was quite correct that she knew nothing of him. It was wise of her to keep her own counsel if she were a noblewoman of any standing. Kidnappings played a valuable part in negotiations between hostile parties. And hostile parties were a distinct possibility in these times.

When the horn had sounded and he had turned to reply, he had almost expected her to abscond. He was surprised by the accord she had issued instead, a challenge to test his honor. It was, of course, unnecessary, for he had been content to let her go at that point, regardless. Nonetheless, it had offered a further clue to her breeding.

As she wheeled away, he watched her go, a thought forming in his mind. He had not established her identity, but something told him that despite her recalcitrance, it might not be long before he did. Then he gathered up his own reins. He had been gone ten minutes from his party when they had sounded their horn. They would expect him back or start to suspect foul play. He rode off to rejoin them.

A quarter of a mile from home, Rosamund brought her horse to a standstill by a little stream. Dismounting and looking down at herself, she brushed off any vestiges of dirt that she could see on her clothes. Then she knelt by the water's edge and cleaned her face and hands. She smoothed her damp hands through her hair, feeling for any stray leaf or moss and picking it out. She cursed herself for being foolish enough to take a shortcut through the woodland so near the road. She was not ignorant of the dangers, but she had heard of no robberies for a while. She had also trusted in her ability to outride any trouble — a supposition that bad luck had undermined. She was still trembling from the whole encounter. She steadied her hands against her hot cheeks, trying to calm herself. She wanted no one to know what had happened. The fact was that she should not have been out riding at all that morning.

The trouble was, she had woken too early. The manor house would shortly come to life, but in the half-light of a pink-tinged dawn, most of its inhabitants had still slumbered. She was unable to fall back to sleep; apprehension about the day to come had started to churn in Rosamund's stomach. She could think of only one way to outwit her fears, and that was the escape of a ride, though she knew that neither her father nor mother would countenance such an idea on this of all mornings. So, rising very softly from her bed, she had dressed quickly and quietly, picked her way stealthily out of her room, and made for the stables.

The stable boys were already up and busy tending to their charges. Appearing at the stable door, Rosamund gestured to a groom forking fresh hay into a stall.

"Could you saddle up Flavian please?"

The groom was a little surprised by her request at such an hour but did as he was bade. Flavian was one of the more excitable coursers in his master's stable, but the groom knew Rosamund to be a good rider. Besides, nobody else was likely to need the horse at this hour. He was also unsurprised by Rosamund's unusual garb, being used to the young lady of the manor wearing a man's riding habit for several years now.

It had always seemed foolish to Rosamund to dress in a fashion that impeded one's activity, and riding in skirts was a nuisance. Thus, from an early age she had begged her father for permission to dress like her brothers so that she could ride unfettered as they did. Her father had laughingly agreed and, as he had never looked anew at the issue, Rosamund had continued to pilfer items from her brothers' wardrobes ever since.

She was astride her mount within a few minutes, trotting out of the opened stable gates, across the moat bridge and tended lawns, and then cantering onward to the heathland surrounding the castle, where she had ridden nearly every week of her life since she was allowed on a horse.

She had wondered when she might ride here, on her father's estate, next. Perhaps never. There was no sound save for the call-

ing of the birds and the soft morning breeze
stirring her hair. The sun was rising, disturbing the early mist that had settled across the
fields in the night. Its orange beams set the
dewdrops sparkling and stirred the birds to
louder accompaniment. The air was crisp
and clear. It was a fine morning for a gallop. Rosamund streaked outward across her
father's land, subsumed in the magical
union of horse and rider, revelling in the
speed. She urged Flavian to jump over
hedgerow, stream, and fallen tree, and he
did his very best for his fearless rider.

Making the most of her stolen freedom,
Rosamund strayed further than she had
intended. The woodland through which the
Western Road passed had offered her a
shortcut back toward home.

She had not been in the forest long when
a sound had caught her attention. She
stiffened and stopped her horse immediately. Listening carefully for a minute or so,
she decided she had misheard and urged
her horse on again. Hearing something
again, she felt a prickling of fear creep over
her, and she had quickened her pace as
much as was possible among the trees,
heading away from the sound. The next moment, she had seen Alexander on horseback,
almost upon her. Her fright had her racing

away as fast as she could. She had intended to continue in the direction of the road, where she could pick up speed, but it was her misfortune for her horse to stumble badly, allowing her skillful pursuer his catch.

Reliving the whole sorry incident, Rosamund felt exhausted. The rush of fear from the confrontation had lent her a surge of nervous energy that had now dissipated and left her drained. At least she needn't worry about her reception back at home. She would be leaving home today, whether in disgrace for her adventuring or not. But she knew it would go better for her to avoid any mention of her forest escapade. So she sat by the trickling stream, listening to familiar birdsong, ordering her thoughts and calming herself enough to avoid any concern over her appearance or demeanor. Then she remounted and continued homeward.

By the brightness of the sun, Rosamund judged that she had been out far too long for her absence to go unnoticed. She was right. As her horse trotted back into the stable courtyard, she was met by the sight of a small cavalcade of horsemen and her mother, the latter flapping a handkerchief and bustling toward her with a frown immediately she saw her daughter.

"Wretched child! I could not find you anywhere when I rose this morning. Look! Your escort has already arrived." Rosamund gazed at the wooden wagon drawn up on the cobbles, the grooms leading circling horses. Then she dismounted with the ease of long experience and handed a stable hand her reins. A feeling of disquiet grew within her.

"I sent the maids to find you, and not one had any success. I knew just where to come when they came back empty-handed," continued her mother. " 'Always on a horse,' I said. 'Out with the lark on her last morning, is my guess.' And here you are to prove me right." She tutted, but from her tone, Rosamund could tell she was not truly angry.

"I crave your pardon, Mother," soothed Rosamund, her voice belying her own inner turmoil. Still looking at the arrivals, she added distractedly: "So early. They must have made progress enough yesterday to pass the night at Bowdale and come on at dawn. The horses look fresh enough, and I cannot imagine they rode through the night. But we expected them midmorning, did we not?"

"Quite so. But here they are, just arrived, nonetheless," said her mother, quite uninterested in Rosamund's suppositions, instead looking up and down with the utmost dissatisfaction at her daughter's appearance.

"And they will be ever less fresh as they wait for you to return from your dawn wanderings, dressed like a peasant. Your father will be having words with you. I would ask what I am to do with you, but after today it's no longer my concern. Now, let us hurry, you must tidy yourself and breakfast before you go." Then she sniffed, dabbing her handkerchief to her face, her expression of annoyance suddenly replaced with one of sadness. "And go you must, though I am sorely sorry to lose you, even when you vex me so."

Rosamund clasped her mother's hand. "You know I wish I could stay."

"Alas, I have had more of you than I ought expect," sighed her mother. "Go you must. It is all arranged."

They looked disconsolately at one another until her mother stiffened her shoulders and started shooing her charge toward the house.

"Thankfully, they've only just arrived and have accepted some sustenance, which gives us a little time. So let us ready you apace, my dear. It speaks ill of us to keep a knight waiting."

"A knight?" echoed Rosamund, with further stirrings of anxiety.

"Yes, of course a knight," said her mother. "The knight leading your escort. Naturally Lord Aelward sends a knight for protection, but, according to your father, it seems he has sent his chief man-at-arms, an honor indeed. Apparently, he had business on the way and agreed to join the escort," Rosamund's mother chattered on. "He is the son of an earl, no less, so you address him as Lord, not Sir, do remember — ah! Here, this must be him."

Rosamund turned to look where her mother pointed. A man was approaching them from the far side of the courtyard. His tall frame was silhouetted by the rising sun, but she already knew whom she would see.

CHAPTER TWO

First Rosamund was flooded with outrage. The stranger who had overpowered her in the wood was standing here in front of her again, in the heart of her own home. After their altercation, it felt like an invasion, and she was furious. Why had he not mentioned in the woods where he was headed? They might have resolved their misunderstanding there and then.

She also felt uneasy: he was a high-ranking knight, come in favor to her father, and she had met him not only riding out alone without permission, but with an exchange of bitter words after leading him to believe his party was under attack. Then she marshaled her thoughts in her own defense. No, he should be the one to feel awkward if anyone should: wrestling an unarmed woman to the ground and accusing her of nefarious intent.

Stopping a yard short of them, the noble

newcomer bowed briefly to Rosamund and her mother.

"Lord Alexander Ringewar, chief man-at-arms to Lord Aelward, Earl of Duloe, at your service."

He straightened back up to his full imposing height. Rosamund was herself a generous height for a woman, but he made her feel as petite as her mother standing beside her.

In contrast to the youthful stable hands darting around them, there was nothing of the boy about this man: he looked every inch the battle-wise chevalier. His physical presence aroused unbidden in Rosamund another, more subtle, cognizance. In the forest, her only thoughts had been for her safety. Now, with that recent encounter divested of such menace, she couldn't help but notice the arresting green of his eyes and that his hair now seemed a warm gold in the sun. She could not deny that he was a handsome man.

She was suddenly conscious of her wild, windblown hair and mannish clothes. For her own part, she told herself, she didn't care overmuch, but she ought to be discomfited on her mother's behalf — introducing her grown daughter while she was dressed in her brother's cast-off riding clothes. It was not the vision of a lady that her parents would care for. Despite the confusion of her thoughts, Rosamund could do little else but greet the approaching knight in a ladylike manner, even if she was hardly presenting the picture to accompany it.

"Lady Margaret Galleia, wife of Lord Edmund," her mother said, then curtseyed. "We are honored to receive you. And may I introduce our daughter, Rosamund, whom you are to escort today."

If Alexander was surprised to see Rosamund again, he didn't show it. He merely nodded his head again in acknowledgment, unsmiling. But his green gaze was firmly upon her.

Rosamund felt a rush of hope. It seemed he was not going to mention their forest escapade to her family.

"Please accept our hospitality in any way it might suit," Lady Galleia said to him. "I hope you have been offered some refreshment at our breakfast table?"

"Thank you. Yes, we have. We already broke fast in Bowdale, but my men will take the chance for a mead in the hall before we depart," Alexander replied. "Ordinarily, they would not, but it seems unlikely we will be leaving promptly," he added in a sterner tone. "Nonetheless, we should depart within the hour if we are to reach tonight's lodging before sundown."

Rosamund's relief at his discretion was tempered by irritation at his manner. She wasn't ready to leave, it was true, but if he intended his remark as a rebuke, she would not accept it. It was he who had delayed them both in the forest. Fortunately, his observation relieved them of the need to engage in any further conversation.

"Quite so," said Margaret graciously. "Then, if you will excuse us, it is time I helped Rosamund ready herself so as not to keep you waiting any further."

"Of course," Alexander replied, bowing again. Rosamund and her mother curtseyed back. As Rosamund straightened up she looked at the knight once again. He met her gaze squarely. Despite her annoyance, something about him made her drop her eyes again quickly, and her heart gave a sudden thud.

"Come now, Rosamund," said her mother, leading her smartly across the courtyard. As they entered the house, Rosamund was then most surprised to hear her mother whisper:

"Such a fine-looking man!"

An hour after her inglorious return, Rosamund stood once again in her father's

31

courtyard, now dressed in a plain but presentable gown and a thick traveling cloak. Her hair was brushed and styled into a long braid, and she wore a wool wimple tucked into her cloak for warmth. Her family surrounded her to bid her farewell.

Rosamund could have been long married with many a child around her skirts, yet it was only on this day that she was finally leaving her childhood home. She considered herself lucky to have had such a long reprieve. She was not the only young woman of her station not to wed until age twenty or more, but it was more the custom for girls to be married younger, as young as fifteen, and betrothed even earlier. Her mother, Margaret, however, with a tendency to ill health, had but one daughter in Rosamund, and she was loath to part with her at such a tender age. Nor did she wish to lose a happy companion who would read to her and entertain her with games and song when she was forced to take to her bed with the rheumatic pains that plagued her.

"You must release the girl, Margaret," Rosamund's father had boomed at her mother one night over dinner, though the conversation had once again reduced his wife to tears. "Or we'll be feeding her into our dotage."

But with the succession of his barony assured by Rosamund's two elder brothers, who had married as well as could be expected, her father could afford to be a little indulgent. Rosamund stayed with her family for a few years longer. Eventually, however, Margaret was persuaded to bow to tradition and release Rosamund to another noble family to further her domestic tutelage. Following that, a marriage would be arranged for her.

"Like the cattle market," one of her elder brothers had mused before his own betrothal, as a procession of eligible maidens had been suggested to him and his family, each with their pedigree discussed and rated.

Rosamund, at that time still playing with her toys and romping in the fields of her father's manor, did not much care for the idea of being sold like livestock, but there was little other option for a girl in her position.

"Could I not become a nun?" Rosamund, aged eleven, had asked her father. The nuns she had seen at the nearby abbey not long ago seemed to her like graceful visions of goodness in their stone sea of tranquillity.

Her father had greeted her childish request with a shout of laughter.

"Your mother fears a husband who will yoke your high spirits, my child, and has likely passed on her worries. But you would better fear an abbess even more. At least in marriage, you have a chance of companionship, an evening by a warm fire, and a good night's sleep in a comfortable bed. I would not abandon a child of mine to a life such as nuns endure."

Rosamund was confused. "But are they not close to God? Is that not what Father Dominicus tells us we should be?"

"I believe in following the will of God, my child," replied her father, "but I do not believe it has to be followed in the cold, sterile tomb of a nunnery. I want you to live your life a little, not sacrifice it. And that is difficult enough for a woman to do." He smiled wistfully. "We need not talk of this for a year or two yet, my child. Be happy. Play on, and dance. I will decide what's best for you in good time."

When that time came, a few years later, he announced his decision to his wife.

"She'll be happy enough at Duloe, perhaps. They have agreed to have her in the spring."

Thus was Rosamund's immediate fate determined. She would leave to serve as a lady-in-waiting to the Earl and Countess of

Duloe, Lord and Lady Aelward.

Entering another noble family's service was a common practice, she knew, intended to foster goodwill between one noble family and their landowning neighbors. In changeable times, when fortunes were secured by military strength and political connections, these alliances were no small matter. Rosamund's rank was lower than a countess might commonly accept for a lady-in-waiting, but it was not unheard of. Rosamund was aware that her father was staunchly loyal to King Stephen, as was Lord Aelward, while the feudal lords of some neighboring manors were not quite so vociferous in their support of the king. Thus, Edmund Galleia's land provided a small, friendly corridor between the capital and Lord Aelward's own land. A strong enough reason for the earl to offer a temporary home to the baron's daughter.

At the age of twenty-two already, Rosamund guessed she would not stay at Duloe long; her father and Lord Aelward would undoubtedly be looking for an adequate match for her soon enough. And an adequate match would be her lot: a husband of similar rank to her own, no better. Her family had few claims or favors due to cause them to expect anything else. She considered it a blessing that her nuptials had been delayed as long as they had been. She had already witnessed many girls younger than her, but of superior rank or political importance, wedded and dispatched to their new husbands' estates, which could be many miles from their own family homes. Unlike the villeins and peasants of a lord's manor, a noblewoman's destiny was not to plough the same furrow from birth to death, but to be pulled from her roots and obliged to set down new ones with her husband's family. She had no say in who her wedded master might be. It was a matter of some luck whether one ended up serving a kindhearted man in marriage, or a brute.

Reminded of this as she stood once more in the courtyard, Rosamund was keenly aware that she would be expected to apply herself mindfully to whatever Lord and Lady Aelward required of her at Duloe, and to submit to being molded into obedient, marriageable material. But there would be enough time to reflect on such matters on her journey. She turned her attention back to her family clustered around her.

"Am I finally to have my stables to myself?" roared her father, having heard the story of her early-morning disappearance.

But he subsumed his daughter in a fierce hug.

Her brothers handed her sweetmeats and gave her jovial encouragement in her new adventures as the servants loaded parcels of food and belongings onto the wooden wagon brought by the escort.

There were tears shed on the women's part as Rosamund stepped into the wagon. Lady Galleia was hopeful that Rosamund would have a warm welcome at Duloe, but even the greatest of reassurances on that matter would not have decreased her sorrow at their parting. Drying her eyes and attempting to be sanguine, she kissed her daughter good-bye and urged her to comport herself as diligently as she could.

Duloe was forty miles to the west of Rosamund's family's estate, itself twenty miles to the west of London.

"It will take us a full day and half a morning more to get there," Alexander had informed Rosamund's parents just before the party left. "We will send a messenger with word upon our safe arrival."

The journey was a tiring one. In the wagon, Rosamund's bones were shaken continually on the rutted tracks that ran through forest, farmland, and pasture.

Alexander Ringewar led the way several yards ahead, with his squire behind him. One mounted soldier followed behind, directly in front of the two-horse wagon and driver, and two other soldiers rode behind.

Inside the wagon, Rosamund was afforded the company of a chaperone, a cheerful Duloe village woman of a good forty years or so by the name of Hawise. She chattered a great deal about her family in the village, the countryside they were passing through — for she had seen little of it herself before — and anything else that came into her head at a moment's notice, including the pockets of drizzly spring weather, from which they were shielded by nothing more than a thick sacking material slung above the wagon on a wooden frame.

"Well, we shall be cleaner by the end of the journey," Hawise joked as the wind blew the rain in onto them despite the cover. They pulled their cloaks and woolen blankets closer around them.

Rosamund feared she was a slight disappointment to her chaperone as a traveling companion: her sadness at leaving her home, combined with the unspoken dangers that made the soldiers' presence necessary, sobered her, and she felt disinclined to talk. But she was grateful for the woman's company and did her best not to leave her entirely without a conversational foil. Hawise seemed encouraged enough by Rosamund's nods and murmurs to keep her conversation rattling cheerfully on in much the same manner as the wagon that jolted them on their way.

"They'll be after finding you a husband at Duloe," Hawise prophesied. "And they won't have much trouble finding one, by the look of you." She winked in friendly fashion at Rosamund, who smiled but inclined her head in modesty.

"I am but the daughter of a baron with a single manor. That and my father's fortunes determine my prospects."

"Ah, yes," Hawise nodded her head sagely. "But I can tell you, dearie, were you a village girl you'd have the pick of the village crop."

"You're too kind," said Rosamund, touched by the compliment. "But I fear there will be no picking for me. And if I had a choice," she added somewhat incautiously, "I might rather choose to remain unmarried."

This elicited a shriek of laughter from Hawise. "Heaven bless her, she don't want a husband," she chuckled. "As if we women would be allowed to manage aught without one. Mind you, after twenty years with my own, I'm not without sympathy, dearie." She laughed again. "Still, it's a wonder how a comely face can warm the coldest of hearts, be it man or woman who protests their indifference."

Rosamund hoped that Hawise's observation was merely an abstract one. With little else to do on the journey, Rosamund's eyes had been repeatedly drawn to the figure of Alexander Ringewar throughout the day, riding ahead of the wagon as he did. She was still affronted by his treatment of her in the forest. Since their second, and more civilized, acquaintance, he had said nothing to her about their highly irregular first meeting that morning. In fact, his whole demeanor so far might have caused her to think that her forest fall had involved another man entirely, had she not been so certain of the details of his countenance and his voice. Granted, there had been no opportunity for him to speak to her of it in private, but his manner was aloof, not even vaguely conciliatory. Rosamund determined to be just as icily polite until an apology was forthcoming. Yet, being entirely unconcerned with his presence was proving impossible; her gaze kept straying to the proud profile of his face when he turned to look left or right. On occasional sorties, when he rode ahead a couple of hundred yards or so to check the path in front of them, as he had been doing when they had first encountered each other, she couldn't help but admire his ease in the saddle. He was obviously an excellent horseman. Little wonder now that she had failed to shake him off in the forest as she might have done most other riders.

He said little to his fellow soldiers, and even less to the women. But Rosamund noted how he would gesture to his squire to ride up beside him. There they would converse and, though Rosamund could not quite hear them, by the gestures and snatches of conversation that floated her way, she guessed Alexander was instructing the young man on some knightly topic or other, as was his duty. The squire's young face would turn to Alexander with expressions of interest and respect — and occasional bursts of laughter. Clearly, the knight was an entertaining teacher.

Finally, as the sun started to set and the sky passed through ever darker shades of indigo, Alexander rode up alongside the wagon.

"We are but a few minutes from our resting place tonight," he informed them. Sure enough, their track soon widened out into the main thoroughfare of a village. There were few people abroad; most were already inside their small dwellings, smoke issuing from the thatched roofs, fires warding off the twilight chill.

The wagon drew to a halt outside one of the larger buildings. Rosamund was very relieved that she had the opportunity to stretch her aching body. Alexander and his squire dismounted swiftly, and Alexander strode across the cobbles to assist the women from the wagon. Ordinarily, Rosamund would not have needed assistance, but the many hours of sitting down and being bumped about had left her cold and stiff. The pain in her side from her fall was also protesting its existence. She took Alexander's offered hand with a murmur of thanks and tried to disguise her wince of discomfort as she stood up straight at last. Hawise, descending next, was far more effusive.

"Why, I feel like a noble lady myself, being offered assistance by such a handsome knight. You do me an honor, sir," she said coquettishly, before adding in an undertone to Rosamund, "Would that I could get a bit closer."

If only you knew, thought Rosamund, her

stomach giving a little flip as her mind flashed back to the events of only a few hours ago, when she had lain on the ground trapped beneath Alexander's unyielding body. She herself had no desire to indulge in unseemly flirtation, but she reflected momentarily on the older woman's bawdy remark. It was notable: first her mother, now Hawise. Clearly this Lord Ringewar had an effect on women, age notwithstanding.

Alexander gave Hawise a brief ghost of a smile as he helped her down, and Rosamund found herself watching the curl of his mouth at the corners and the flicker of warmth in his eyes, only the first instance of it she had seen since she had met him. *So there is a little humor in there,* she thought.

Alexander ushered Rosamund and Hawise into the inn to a rough-hewn table, and in amiable but decisive tones he ordered some food from the innkeeper. The innkeeper was already jumping to serve, having seen the visitors arriving.

"My wife has prepared rooms, as you requested on your way through," he informed Alexander in a respectful voice.

Once assured that all the necessary arrangements were in place, Alexander left Rosamund and Hawise to await their meal, saying he must see to the soldiers and check on the stabling. Rosamund was unsurprised. Knights took a fierce interest in the welfare of their chargers. Their fate could rest upon the strength and fitness of their horse as much as on their own military skill, while the amount of time a knight spent in equine pursuits on a daily basis could not help but forge strong bonds between rider and steed. With an indifferent nod of acknowledgement, Rosamund watched as the inscrutable knight excused himself from their company.

Their meal was merely a stew, but it was hot, salty, and substantial. To Rosamund, it was delicious, and she could feel it warming her up from the inside out. As the shadows had lengthened toward the end of the day's travel, the air had chilled, and even the blankets that the wagon had been stocked with could not entirely banish the cold that settles on the bones of seated travelers who cannot warm themselves as they would on a brisk walk. A fire also burned in a grate a few yards away from them. It warmed the room pleasantly and, along with the tallow candles the innkeeper was now lighting, provided light to hold the gloom of the descending night at bay.

As Hawise and Rosamund ate, the inn door opened again. Looking up, Rosamund assumed it would be Alexander and the other soldiers, but instead she saw two unfamiliar men. She guessed them to be in their forties and, from their dress, not noblemen, but perhaps merchants. They were past their prime for certain but not, she thought as she observed their demeanor, past the ability to cause trouble. Loudly demanding full tankards of ale from the innkeeper, they proceeded to seat themselves at a table close to Rosamund and Hawise. Perhaps merely to warm themselves at the fire, thought Rosamund, but she still felt disquiet at their proximity. The men had a rambunctious air about them, a seeming intention to make merry and not mind if they caused anyone else annoyance or discomfort. In a strange place, Rosamund felt suddenly vulnerable. She found herself studiously avoiding eye contact with the men, as did Hawise, with a warning glance to the younger woman. It was to no avail though. Rosamund had guessed their mood correctly, and when their eyes lit upon her, a vivacious young woman seemingly without a male companion, it was merely a minute or two before they set after their quarry.

"A good evening to you," said one, a bony man with a sunken face and balding pate, as he leaned over toward them. His words were civil enough, but the unpleasant leer on his face belied his initial politeness. "Have you traveled far?"

She and Hawise could affect not to hear them, thought Rosamund, but she suspected the men might not take to this kindly.

"Too shy to answer?" asked the other, a fatter, bibulous man, having hardly given them a chance to do so. "Or do you not like the look of us?" He turned to his companion. "I don't think they like the look of us, else why don't they speak?"

"We come from thirty miles hence," said Hawise briefly, to mollify them.

Rosamund knew they had fallen into the trap of being forced to speak lest they foster yet more antagonism.

"Ah, one speaks," said the first man. "Not so shy after all."

His patronizing tone riled Rosamund, but she knew there was no sense in taking overt exception to it. Better to wait it out and hope they soon got bored.

"Does the young lady speak too?" He turned his unwelcome gaze upon Rosamund.

"The young lady is tired," said Hawise, to distract him.

"Ah," said the man with mock sympathy, "but not too tired for five minutes of conversation surely, such a young and spritely lass. Where are you headed, my dear?"

"Duloe Manor," Rosamund muttered.

"The new castle," said the portly man. "We have a noble lady on our hands here, my friend. Though we could tell that from her pretty clothes, couldn't we?"

"That we could," said the first.

Rosamund could feel them undressing her with their eyes. It was deliberately disrespectful, but there was nothing she could do about it.

"So, off to your marriage bed is my guess," said the thinner man again, and they both fell into paroxysms of ribald laughter.

Rosamund flushed but didn't speak. She was furious, but also intimidated.

"Your conversation is most ungentlemanly." Hawise spoke up to chide them, but they paid her no heed.

"Well, if she cares for a little practice tonight," said the second man, "we'd be more than happy to offer our services."

They both roared with laughter again. The thinner man stretched out an arm and, to Rosamund's disconcertion, stroked her hair with his fingers. She jerked away from him, and, when he tried to touch her again, batted his arm away with her own. His amusement turned sour; the lewd smile vanished, to be replaced with a look of beady-eyed belligerence. Rosamund met his eyes with a stony glare. Ignoring them had not worked: she would try brazen hostility.

"Touch me again, and you will regret it."

She could see the man's face redden. He began to rise from his seat. "I don't think I'd regret it at all, pretty one." Then, oddly, he froze and went silent.

"You men seek to insult a lady," came a voice from behind her.

Rosamund had been so absorbed by the confrontation that she had failed to see Alexander Ringewar enter the inn once more. He had come upon them with admirable stealth for so large a man, but his presence was certainly noticeable when he spoke. His squire had also entered the inn and was standing by the door. Alexander towered above the two seated men, his face like granite, his garb and mail an added sign of the trouble he might cause them. The men rose to their feet, but Alexander still had the advantage in both height and brooding menace.

"We were just engaging in conversation," stuttered the first. "Getting to know our fellow travelers."

"The ladies do not wish to make your acquaintance." Alexander's voice was as cold as his expression. "And your conversation, what little I heard of it, was a disgrace."

The men shifted uneasily on their feet. They had also spotted Alexander's squire standing by the entrance.

Alexander rested his hand lightly on his sword handle. The action did not go unnoticed by the two unhappy men.

"I believe you owe the lady an apology," he said, nodding toward Rosamund.

The men obviously decided to follow the path of least resistance.

"If you say so, of course," said the first. "Sorry my dear, if you took our jesting badly." His eyes flicked nervously to Rosamund and then back to Alexander.

Alexander stared meaningfully at the other man.

"My apologies also," the fatter man muttered, bowing his head in the women's direction.

"Now, as I can see you have finished here," said Alexander, looking at their almost full tankards, "you'll want to be on your way as quickly as possible."

"But — but we rest the night here," said the second man, momentarily incautious in his dismay at leaving the warmth of the inn at so late an hour.

"You will not spend a restful night here,"

Alexander said calmly, "unless it would rest you to feel the flat of my sword."

Clearly it did not, as neither man spoke again. Instead, they gathered up their belongings sulkily and headed for the door, Alexander's eyes still upon them.

"Thank you, my lord," said Rosamund as he eventually turned back to the women. Disinclined as she had been to feel kindly toward him, she could not help but be relieved at his intervention.

"Yes, thank you indeed," said Hawise more enthusiastically. "Why, it was a good thing you came in when you did, for they were determined to sport with our lady here. They had an air about them right from the start that told us they would as soon turn to malice as any other mood."

"I saw them arrive," said Alexander, "and thought a closer inspection would not be amiss; my instincts coincided with your own. I only regret I did not come sooner."

"Your diligence is most appreciated, my lord," said Hawise. "And why, they were like frightened kittens when you challenged them, the cowards."

She positively beamed at this, and Rosamund nodded her agreement, turning to Hawise and adding, "And thank you too, Hawise, for speaking up for me."

"No thanks are due to me, dearie. You were bold enough. It was only ale, by my reckoning, that stopped them from thinking twice at your tone. I'd gamble sixpence they'd been in a tavern already, and there's no reasoning with a drunkard."

"I will witness their departure, then return," said Alexander. He gestured to his squire. "William here will keep you company."

"They could have done with a hiding, my lord," Rosamund heard the squire say as Alexander approached him.

"They offered no resistance," replied Alexander, pushing open the inn door. "A knight does not fight unless he needs to. Had they laid a hand on the women, it would have been another matter. They would have received a beating without a moment's hesitation."

By the time Alexander returned, the women had finished their supper and Hawise declared them ready to retire. Alexander and William escorted them to their room.

At first, as she lay on her bed that night, Rosamund could not sleep. Aside from the contented snores of Hawise and the lumpiness of her palliasse, she was filled not merely with the natural anxiety of leaving home but now agitation from the supper-time confrontation. She felt deeply un-settled. The uncertainty of the days ahead kept her mind whirling. The encounter had illustrated to her in no uncertain terms how vulnerable a woman was to any manner of unwelcome behavior if she were not under a man's protection. A coarse conversation was the least of it, she knew. She fidgeted in her bed as if her body were trying to do the work of ridding her mind of its discomfort. She tried to calm herself a little. Nothing deplorable had happened. The reality was not just that there were unpleasant men to beware of, but that her father had seen to it that she was protected from any danger with an escort duly capable of that task. And then, creeping into her thoughts, came the dark golden head of Alexander Ringewar. She recalled his easy mastery of the situa-tion. She had to admit her gratitude to him even though he acted merely as he had been charged to. Her icy resolve to hold his morning's actions against him wavered. Her anxiety abating a little, exhaustion captured her, and she slept.

CHAPTER THREE

It did not seem a moment before Hawise was gently shaking her shoulder to wake her. After they had dressed, William arrived to escort them to breakfast. Rosamund only saw Alexander again as she and her chaperone were finishing their meal. Entering the hostelry, he came over to their table. The sun shone through a window onto his corn-colored hair and glinted off his mail. The low ceiling emphasized his height.

"Good morning. I trust you slept well." His voice was clipped, but his tone cordial.

"Yes, thank you," replied Rosamund, declining to mention the worries and discomforts that had robbed her of the first part of her night's rest. "I trust you rested well also," she added.

He looked a little surprised to be asked. Perhaps battle-hardened knights did not think of the comfort of their sleep, Rosamund reflected. She wondered where he had slept; the inn was small, and it was entirely possible he had spent the night in the stables.

"Quite adequately, thank you."

The rest of their conversation was just as brief. Alexander excused himself, saying he would come to fetch Rosamund and Hawise when the wagon and soldiers were readied for the remainder of the journey.

Where it could, the bumpy road they took that morning followed the twisting hedgerows of farmed land. For the last few miles of the journey, however, they had to go once again into the dense forest that covered so much of the realm. The tangled trees cast a gloom on the narrow track, allowing little sunlight through their canopy.

Traveling through heavily wooded regions was always a more dangerous part of a journey, Rosamund knew, for forests were a haven for those who fled the harsh law of the land or who wished to earn a dishonest living robbing the richer travelers who passed their way. She had not been sent an armed escort merely out of courtesy. The forest's dim, watchful atmosphere added to her apprehension.

She was aware that the country was also presently suffering under the instability of the reign of King Stephen. A just and fair man, her father had said from his limited acquaintance with the monarch. But Stephen was hamstrung by the ongoing struggle with his cousin Matilda for the throne and, as the years passed since the death of Matilda's father, Henry, the nobility were becoming increasingly lawless. It was not just a question of divided loyalties among the nobility regarding which royal's claim to support. Without strong rule from the royal court, feudal lords were free to rule their small fiefdoms as they saw fit. Less scrupulous magnates were taking the opportunity of such weak rule to take control of swathes of land that were not legally theirs, to build castles and raise armies without permission, and to ignore taxation and regulations that should have held their power in check. In response, other noblemen were arming themselves and fortifying their positions as defensive measures against potential aggression from their ambitious neighbors. A merciful king was one thing, but a weak, challenged monarch was quite another.

Hawise seemed to sense Rosamund's tension, for she stretched out a hand and placed it over Rosamund's own with a little squeeze. "Don't worry, my pet. Our escort could see off any ill-doers, if that's what you're thinking."

Rosamund was grateful for the comfort. Yesterday, she now discovered, had left her with a heightened awareness of the possibility of an unfriendly encounter.

Fortunately, whether by luck or due to the visible deterrent of the men-at-arms, the party did not encounter any trouble. Rosamund's rumbling fears faded from her mind and were replaced with a different anticipation as her destination grew near. They emerged out of the woodland and back into open farmland. The countryside of the Earl of Duloe's extensive manors lay ahead, bathed in glorious sunshine. This was fertile, bountiful farming land, wetter than the eastern counties but warmer than more northerly shires.

Duloe Castle came into sight as soon as they broke from the forest; an imposing, thick-walled fortress with tall keep and stone bailey, atop a broad rise that formed part of a backbone of gentle hills and upland extending north to south across Lord Aelward's land. The castle's high walls were the warm honey color of local stone. As they drew closer, Rosamund could see the final defensive fortifications to the bailey still in progress: the completion of the castellation atop the incredibly thick stone outer walls and the excavation of a still-dry moat. Spread out below the castle and its hills on the lee side to the east was the beautiful Lyn valley: acres of meadow, pasture, and farming land, with the River Lowen winding through it. On the southeastern side of the castle sat an old manor house. Further down the slope lay the closest village of the manor, with a host of wooden dwellings and a small church of the same honey-colored stone as the manor house and castle.

A swath of pasture and agricultural land extended outward from the village: here the serfs and peasants toiled to make a living for themselves as well as pay their taxes in pennies and goods to the church and to their liege. Behind the castle to the west lay mile upon mile of thick forest of oak and ash, similar to that which Rosamund had just passed through.

Life was harsh for the commoners on any manor, but at a distance the splendor of the landscape concealed the daily realities of its inhabitants. Rosamund could, at that moment, only bear witness to its rich beauty as it paraded the bright green promise of the warmer seasons ahead. As her little wagon creaked on up the track to the manor house itself, she could only pray that she would share a little of the joys of the buds bursting into bloom and the birds freewheeling in the sky.

As the small cavalcade made its way into the manor-house courtyard, servants and stable boys hurried out to meet it. Drawing to a halt, Alexander Ringewar dismounted from his horse, and Rosamund found him once again standing in front of her to help her step down from the wagon. Ever the chivalrous knight, she observed, even if he speaks little. She was in no need of assistance this morning, since they had not traveled half as far as the day before, but she took his hand anyway, out of politeness. Even with the multitude of new sights and sounds to absorb, she momentarily found herself sympathizing with Hawise's playful response to Alexander the previous evening — something about this tall knight's brief attention to her welfare gratified her. His hand was bare and brown, and she could feel the warmth and strength of it as she placed her own within it.

Her attention was suddenly diverted by a flurry of bows and curtsies from the waiting staff as two more people entered the courtyard. Rosamund guessed they must be Lord Aelward and Lady Iolanthe.

"Alexander, my friend," called the lord, striding toward them. "I trust your journey was untroubled."

Rosamund wondered if she heard a hesitation in Alexander's voice before he replied.

"We had no trouble on the roads. We encountered two undesirable types at our lodgings, but they were easily dealt with."

"Thieves?"

"Mere drunkards."

"Ah. Well, I'm glad there was nothing else to test you," said Lord Aelward. "But I must tell you, even in your short absence there have been developments here. Lord Parnell is overstepping his mark again, curse him. I grow ever less convinced we will see out the year in peace. But I forget my manners," he cried, turning to Rosamund, beckoning with an outstretched arm as she waited behind Alexander to be greeted.

"My dear Rosamund, a joy to have you here. My wife has been looking forward to your company ever since this plan to bring you here was formed."

"It's most kind of you to accommodate me. I am greatly looking forward to my sojourn here," replied Rosamund, warmed by his generous welcome.

"Rosamund, my dear." Lady Iolanthe, in her turn, held out her arms and embraced

Rosamund. She drew back and held Rosamund at arm's length. "Yes," she nodded. "You will do quite nicely." She beamed kindly at her.

Lord Aelward addressed Rosamund again.

"And of course you will now be acquainted with my chief man-at-arms, Lord Ringewar.

"This noble knight here," continued Lord Aelward, "was once my squire. I am quite certain I would not be here today were it not for him steadfast at my side these last ten years."

"Then I am most grateful to him, my lord," said Rosamund.

"Your Lordship does me great service by such a proclamation," said Alexander. "Every honorable man does his best by the other, and it is more than likely the other way round."

"You are too modest, sir," said Lord Aelward, clapping him on the shoulder and addressing him in the manner that a liege would his knight. "But here, I am doing nothing but delaying you a proper welcome to my home. Let me do that, at least."

"I will not be stopping long," said Alexander, as they proceeded across the cobbles. "I must return to my brother's estate for a while. Merely some business matters, but it must be done. I intend to depart again in a day or so, when my horse is rested."

"Then you and I have much to discuss in the next hours, my friend," replied Lord Aelward, his face suddenly serious. "Perhaps you will take supper with me in my study, where we can discuss the wretched matter of Parnell in more depth."

Anticipating a parting of ways as they reached the heavy oak doors of the house, Rosamund had only a brief chance to address her thanks to Alexander for escorting her to Duloe.

His green eyes rested upon her face for a moment.

"I hope your stay at Duloe will be a happy one," he said simply. Then he and her uncle were gone, out of sight into the depths of the house.

Rosamund herself was ushered away by Lady Iolanthe and the servants to her new quarters in the manor house.

"We all still reside down here at present," Iolanthe said to her as they walked along a stone-flagged corridor. "The castle is but newly built, as you may know. My lord will have us move up there in good time, but he has given me grace to rest as we are down here for the summer — unless trouble happens upon us, of course. And I shall count this summer a blessing, for it will be chaos, utter chaos, when we uproot ourselves for good. Though perhaps no more than the chaos we have suffered year upon year during the building of the blessed thing. Up here, my dear," she added as they arrived at the bottom of a wooden staircase.

"My first task will be to establish the adequacy of the fires, of that there will be no doubt," said Iolanthe with fervor, climbing upward. "The winter wind chills my bones, Rosamund. I am gladder than you can imagine to be shaking it off now that spring is come." She gave a mock shudder of disgust at the weather and its tiresome ways.

Rosamund smiled. She was already warming to this chatterbox of a woman, whose manner was a considerable relief: Rosamund knew that not all ladies-in-waiting were treated well. During her travels to other noblemen's manors in the past she had seen the way that some young women were treated by their hosts. Some worked long hours without rest for their mistress, were spoken to harshly, and were punished for trifling transgressions. If the lady of the manor was unpleasant, it inevitably followed that life would be so for her ladies-in-waiting. While it would seem illogical for a girl to be badly treated when the object of her stay was to foster good relations between her family and her host's, communication and travel were poor and infrequent enough that a girl in an unhappy household had little chance to inform her family of her plight. A letter could be read before it was taken by a messenger, and things might go badly for the sender if the mistress of the house became aware of any content that besmirched her good name among her neighbors. With this in mind, Iolanthe's twinkling eyes and happy countenance boded well.

"Let me take you to meet the rest of the household," Iolanthe beckoned. "They wait in the solar."

Rosamund found herself being ushered by Iolanthe into a large room with south-facing windows, which allowed the bright sun of the spring day to flood in. The solar had a generous number of comfortable-looking chairs and benches upon which the other women were seated. They rose as one at Iolanthe and Rosamund's appearance. Despite a twinge of shyness, Rosamund was practiced enough in etiquette to be able to summon up a gracious smile and meet their curious gazes.

"My dear ladies," announced Iolanthe. "I am delighted to introduce Rosamund Galleia, daughter of Lord Edmund Galleia of Osburn. She will reside with us now until marriage. We must do our very best to make her welcome. Now, Rosamund, let me acquaint you with the rest of my family."

First Iolanthe introduced Alice Gregory, Lord Aelward's widowed sister, a woman of similar age to Iolanthe. She was slight of figure, affable looking, and had graying hair. Softly spoken, she asked Rosamund if she had had a tolerable journey. Not wishing to make too much of the previous night's disagreeableness, Rosamund merely murmured, "Yes, quite adequate, thank you."

"Save for drunkards at the lodging house," interjected Iolanthe. "Lord Ringewar mentioned it but briefly in the courtyard. Pray, what did he mean?"

Rosamund reluctantly recounted the story.

"Heavens!" murmured Alice.

"Gracious!" exclaimed Iolanthe. "What a traveling woman must face. One would think they would know better when they saw a lady of rank. You must have been frightened, my dear."

"It was really nothing of consequence," insisted Rosamund. "Lord Ringewar dispatched them with little trouble."

"I'm sure he did," agreed Lady Iolanthe. "I would put my faith in him every time. Such a man of duty. I raised him from a page, you know."

Rosamund could simply not imagine the towering Alexander as a seven-year-old boy.

"But we digress," said Iolanthe. She proceeded to introduce Rosamund to Milicent, wife of Robert, the Aelward's only son, and heir to the Duloe estate.

As she met Milicent's gaze, Rosamund saw no friendliness in the dark eyes; rather, she was scrutinized by an overlong stare before Milicent's mouth curved into a smile that never mustered the enthusiasm to reach her eyes. Rosamund knew that first impressions could be misleading, but the other young woman's subtle demeanor did not stir Rosamund to liking.

Then Iolanthe turned to an apple-cheeked, flaxen-haired young woman who bobbed a neat curtsy to Rosamund and beamed at her. Iolanthe introduced her as Lady Maud Hughes, the as-yet-unmarried daughter of an earl in the west country. Rosamund's mood was buoyed up again by the sight of Maud. Again, she could not judge entirely on first impressions, but something about Maud's open, smiling face made Rosamund warm to her and wonder if she might find a friend in Maud where she would not with Milicent. Time would tell.

The final figure in the room Iolanthe introduced as Godith Wetherall, a cousin of Lord Aelward's through his mother, and lady-in-waiting to Alice Gregory. Godith was petite, pallid of complexion, and mousy haired. Rosamund guessed she was not in the first flush of youth but certainly not beyond her childbearing years.

Godith almost stumbled as she and Rosamund curtsied to each other, and her mumbled greeting was so quiet that Rosamund could hardly hear it. She seemed painfully shy, avoiding Rosamund's eyes. Rosamund gave her a wide smile, resisting a sudden urge to give the poor creature a hug and assure her that she, Rosamund, did not bite.

After the introductions were complete, Iolanthe turned to Maud with a request.

"Would you be a dear and provide Rosamund a reconnaissance of the house before dinner?"

"It would be my pleasure, my lady," replied Maud, her flaxen curls bouncing as she curtsied to her aunt and then offered her arm to Rosamund, who took it, pleased at her aunt's choice of guide.

Rosamund had to admit that the manor house was a handsome home and as comfortable as any she had seen. On the first floor, where they started from, there were several private chambers for members of the family. Maud led her first into the smallest.

"The unmarried women sleep here."

Rosamund looked about her. The furniture consisted of four low beds, a wardrobe, a small washtable in one corner, and a shelf with a few books and trinkets upon it. There was rough matting on the wooden floor. Woven hangings broke up the pale daub of the walls. Servants had already brought up Rosamund's clothes and possessions and laid them on the bed closest to the room's sole window. The window was narrow, in keeping with the protection the house needed to provide, but the wooden shutters were thrown back, letting a shaft of sunlight stream in and affording a view to the west. Looking beyond the courtyard and over the retaining wall, Rosamund could see grassed lawns that gave way downhill to acres of green forest.

Maud had time to point out the bower, garderobe, wardrobe, and family chapel before a bell sounded from the direction of the courtyard.

"Dinner," said Maud happily, turning on one heel and motioning to Rosamund to follow. "You must be hungry after your journey."

Rosamund had forgotten her appetite in the newness of everything, but at the thought of food, she realized she was indeed ravenous.

Maud led the way, along the upper corridor with its woven tapestries and ornate candles in their sconces, and back down the staircase to the ground floor. Thence they made their way along another corridor until they arrived at the top end of the Great Hall. Servants curtsied respectfully as they entered. Maud stepped onto a raised wooden dais with a long table upon it where the lord, his family, and visiting nobility sat. Two other tables ran perpendicular to it along the length of the hall. Between them in the center of the hall was a shallow square pit for a fire, presently empty due to the warmth of the day. Above their heads, the roof, with its huge vaulted oak beams, stretched away to the same height as the rooms on the first floor.

The hall filled up rapidly with manor-house and castle staff until there must have been fifty people or more. Those of higher rank sat closest to the dais, those lower at the farther end, toward the kitchens. Maud nudged Rosamund from time to time and identified sundry people for her.

"There is Drake, the seneschal," she whispered, her eyes pointing toward a gangly, dour-looking man. "He's not so bad really, but terribly grumpy. He is always annoyed by the housekeeper, for she finds everything amusing. That's her there." Maud pointed to a large woman with a full apron over her skirts. "Brunhilde. I do like her, though I confess she has shocked me on occasion with some of the things she says." Maud blushed with some unknown recollection, but said no more, leaving Rosamund intrigued.

Of another man, short and black haired, Maud whispered: "That's the constable. Now that the castle is nearly finished, we see less of him and the men-at-arms, for they reside up there now. He has what he thinks is a secret fondness for the wardrobe mistress, but he will see far less of her now. I think he will be heartbroken unless he can pluck up the courage to address her." She winked, and Rosamund giggled.

"There she is." Maud nodded over to a woman whom Rosamund presumed was the wardrobe mistress in question. "She is very sweet, actually," said Maud. "Far too sweet to tell me that my embroidery is hopeless and I should try harder at it. And far too shy to admit whether she in turn likes the constable."

Maud continued in this fashion while Rosamund listened in bemused fascination, until there was a scraping back of benches as everybody stood up to acknowledge the entrance of Lord and Lady Aelward, Milicent, and a man who, Rosamund presumed, must be Lord Robert. They were preceded by a chaplain and followed by Alexander Ringewar in his distinctive hauberk. The chaplain said grace, after which Lord and Lady Aelward sat down and the rest followed suit. From the kitchens, servants began to file out, arms laden with bowls of food.

As they ate, Rosamund was unable to see any but her immediate companions on the dais from their identical positions facing down the hall, but as she looked around, absorbing the scene and the faces, she noticed a serving girl looking in the direction of the dais on more than one occasion. Craning her neck surreptitiously, she looked to see where the girl's attention was focused. It was clearly on Alexander Ringewar. Another who notices his good looks, she thought.

"Lord Ringewar led your escort, did he not?" Maud nodded toward Alexander and continued on her amorous theme. "I'm afraid I can reveal no confidences regarding him. He is the chivalrous knight in extremis; either that, or he is unerringly discreet. Rarely does a summer go by when one of our visitors does not find herself quite taken with him, but never does he stir to anything past a mild benevolence."

"Indeed?" Rosamund replied noncommittally. In their short acquaintance, mild benevolence was certainly the very warmest she could ascribe to Alexander. She was also instantly resolved not to give Maud cause to include her as a woman so obviously distracted by the knight.

"Neither is there a shortage of families suggesting a daughter of theirs he might wed," continued Maud, "but he has shown no interest through all the time I have been here. It is most vexing to them, Lady Iolanthe tells me."

"And how many summers have you been here?" Rosamund asked, determined not to imply any interest in Alexander by pursuing a conversation about him.

"Two years just gone." And with little prompting, Maud began to speak of her own arrival at Duloe.

As she returned her attention to her meal of vegetables and mutton, Rosamund realized her linen napkin had dropped to the floor. With no servant immediately on hand, she twisted around to retrieve it herself. Turning back, she saw Alexander observing her movement from along the row of people that separated them. Maud's pleasant chatter faded momentarily into the background as their eyes met. But Alexander merely gave her a terse nod before turning back to his food. His unsmiling manner stung Rosamund a little. Why had she glanced at him at all, she chastised herself. Even without intending to, she might appear as immodest as that serving girl. Had Maud's words of only moments ago taught her nothing of how easy it might be to make a fool of herself in a household that, like most others, clearly thrived upon gossip? Shaking her head almost imperceptibly, she turned back to Maud and her lighthearted commentary. Alexander Ringewar, with his austere disposition, would be gone in a day or two and would be of little concern to her.

So why, she realized with a little chill, did the thought of his absence dispirit her?

Chapter Four

In the weeks following her arrival, and Alexander's summary departure, Rosamund had not had cause to change her opinions from those she had formed on her initial meeting with her new female companions at Duloe. She liked Milicent none the better on closer acquaintance. Milicent, she learned, was twenty-four years of age and had been married to Robert for six years, during which time she had produced both a young son and heir, and a daughter. To Rosamund's eyes, Milicent, a dark-haired, thin young woman, was attractive enough, but in a sharp, pinched sort of way. Rosamund found her altogether too quick to find fault on any occasion and to seize on an unflattering interpretation of an event when there might have been one more positive.

By virtue of her connections, Milicent had spent a little time at the royal court before her marriage. Rosamund found Milicent's continual harking to the fashions of Court, the intrigues of Court, and the general superiority of all persons at Court a little wearing. Milicent's matrimonial ambitions were fulfilled well enough when she married Robert, but she regularly implied — out of Iolanthe's earshot — that life was lacking at Duloe in comparison to the sophistication of London. Rosamund discovered quickly that Milicent was at her happiest when visitors arrived from London and its environs with whom she could gossip about the latest clothes, betrothals, and scandals. Iolanthe had a keen ear for gossip herself, but Rosamund found Milicent's commentaries on the latest happenings always more critical than Iolanthe's merry chatter. Try as she might, Rosamund could not like her.

And in reciprocity, Rosamund had the strong suspicion that Milicent was not particularly enthusiastic to consort with someone on a daily basis who ranked below her on the social scale.

"You must feel a little out of place," Milicent had said to her, with no attempt to reassure Rosamund that she wasn't. Fortunately, Rosamund did not suffer much in that regard. She knew she had a right through kinship to be at Duloe even if her rank was inferior, and she said as much. Milicent's raising of a dubious eyebrow only increased Rosamund's suspicions of snobbery, but she refused to satisfy Milicent by feeling out of her element. The scale of her new world was a little larger and a few aspects of life — such as the meals and the clothes and the rank of some visitors — were grander, but most facets of her new life remained unchanged.

Milicent had responded to Rosamund's calm assertion of this by saying, "Well, I must admit Duloe is a little provincial. I can see where the similarities would lie."

Their relationship had not warmed as the weeks went by.

Fortunately, Rosamund found the rest of her daily companions pleasant company. Her Aunt Iolanthe was a delight, Alice Gregory a most agreeable woman, and Godith as quiet and inoffensive as she could make herself. Maud quickly proved an eager ally, and Rosamund was glad of her warm welcome.

In contrast to his wife, Rosamund had also warmed immediately to Lord Robert, the Aelward's only son. His sisters, already married, had moved away, east of the capital and too far distant to visit more than occasionally. Robert, however, as was common for the inheriting child, still resided at the manor house. At twenty-seven he was older than Rosamund, but she liked him a good deal. Conscientious, he took his future position as lord of the manor seriously and was often to be found in discussion with the castle steward over the revenue from their estate or the adequacy of last year's harvests. Trained as a knight in the traditional manner, he was competent in the saddle but not a natural warrior. He was more inclined toward the scholarly arts, and as he was thus well educated and extensively read, Rosamund found him an interesting conversationalist.

She did wonder if part of Milicent's animosity toward her was in part because she and Robert had fallen into so easy a companionship. This had been quickly cemented by the horse rides they had starting taking together. To her relief, Alexander had clearly said nothing to the Aelwards of his and Rosamund's own particular equine escapade, and Rosamund had been greatly pleased when her uncle had given her permission to ride at Duloe.

"We shan't deprive you of it, fear not," he had assured her one evening after supper when she had plucked up the courage to ask. "I understand more ladies are riding for pleasure these days. But I do insist you ride accompanied. What do you think, Lady Aelward, shall we have you out on horseback too, my dear?"

Iolanthe tutted good-naturedly at her husband as she rested in her rocking chair.

"If you care for a wife with a broken leg and will come to find me in the nearest ditch where I have fallen, I will oblige you, but it is not from my own desire, I can assure you."

"Very well, you may stay on firm land. Though I would have enjoyed the sight of it, I must say. Ha!" Lord Aelward chuckled at his vision of his plump wife at the trot.

"You ride, do you, Rosamund?" asked her cousin Robert, who was standing by the window, watching men in a distant field finish their work for the day. The pink sky augured another sunny day to follow, but the young crops could have done with a drop of rain.

"Yes," Rosamund replied, beaming at him. "Since I was very young. After I hounded my older brothers long enough, they took pity on me and taught me."

"Well, I intend to take a ride tomorrow morning myself," said Robert, smiling at her youthful enthusiasm. "Would you care to join me?"

Rosamund was thrilled. "I would be delighted — but only if I can be spared." She turned to her aunt for her verdict, her eyes already shining eagerly.

Iolanthe smiled. "I can spare you. But you will need a chaperone." It was not a personal judgment on either of them: convention dictated that an unmarried woman could not ride alone with a man.

Rosamund looked around beseechingly. Iolanthe would not ride, and without a doubt Milicent would not offer. Maud, she knew, could not ride and would not have been a suitable chaperone in any case due to her age. It was Lady Gregory who stepped into the breach.

"I am not an accomplished rider by any stretch of the imagination," she warned, "but I would be happy to make up the threesome if the other parties will forgive my slowness."

The other parties were quite happy with this — except Milicent, who pursed her lips disapprovingly.

"Splendid. Thank you, Alice," said Iolanthe. "But take good care of them, Robert. Rosamund's riding career will be short-lived if there are any injuries. We are responsible to her father."

"Of course, Mother. Though if my cousin

has been riding since she was a child, I wouldn't fear too much for her safety. Am I right, Rosamund?"

Rosamund could see Milicent was not pleased with the arrangement, but as long as Robert was happy with it, Milicent could not stop them.

After proving her capability on their first outing, her cousin permitted Rosamund to ride any of his hunters, all with a good turn of speed. Rosamund had not dared ask of her uncle if she could wear men's riding clothes, but instead donned a pair of men's hose under her skirts so as to maintain her modesty. If Alice had noticed her skirts flying out to reveal them on their first morning ride, she did not mention it.

A week later, Rosamund and Robert rode together again. It was a blustery day, the blue sky attempting to hold its own against scudding clouds. Alice Gregory chaperoned them once more. She was indeed a much slower rider, sitting as she did in an awkward sidesaddle on which she literally faced outward from her plodding mount. Rosamund wanted to laugh. It was hardly what she would call riding, and she had rejected it outright when it had been suggested to her on her first visit to the Duloe stables.

But with a generosity of spirit, Alice professed herself quite happy on this occasion to let Robert and Rosamund gallop on ahead if they would wait for her at intervals. Rosamund had discovered she was easily a confident enough rider to match Robert's pace, and in a life in which she rarely saw women trained or educated to a point at which they could outshine a man, Rosamund took secret pride in being an accomplished horsewoman.

After nearly an hour's riding, they broke from the forest edge. A mile of smooth grassland stretched between them and the manor house.

Rosamund couldn't resist asking.

"Would you care to race home?" she called to Robert.

He raised his eyebrows a little but accepted the challenge. "I see no reason why not, if Lady Gregory does not mind."

Lady Gregory cheerfully assented to being left behind once again.

"Very well," said Robert. "The oak by the stables will make a good finishing point." Without further word they kicked their steeds into action, urging them to gallop as fast as they could. It was a close-run contest. The thundering of their mounts' hooves rang in their ears as they swept across the grass toward the house. As they came within a couple hundred yards of the stable forecourt they were still neck and neck, and if her cousin showed no sign of slowing down, then Rosamund determined that neither would she. The horses were slick with sweat, their riders both bent low across their horses' withers, urging their mounts to do their utmost. As they swept past the old oak tree not fifty yards from the stone wall of the stable courtyard, Rosamund's bay had just inched ahead of Robert's handsome black, and she threw back her head and laughed in delight at her victory.

"By Heaven, the lady can ride," said Robert, seemingly impressed rather than annoyed by Rosamund's victory. "Well, I daresay I shall let you claim victory, if only to keep you happy." He winked good-naturedly at her and then, before Rosamund could protest, he was turning around to say, "And here comes Lady Gregory. She has been quite an angel to put up with us."

Stable hands came out to meet them, taking their reins as they dismounted. One offered Rosamund his hand to assist her, but she waved him away with a smile and jumped down by herself. As she dusted herself down she suddenly saw a tall figure standing by the gate, watching her with a steady gaze.

Alexander Ringewar had returned.

Robert had by this time swung off his own horse and handed his reins to a groom, and he was striding toward the knight to greet him.

"Lord Alexander," he called. "How fortuitous we should return just as you arrive."

Before she could temper her reaction, Rosamund felt a wave of unexpected self-consciousness at seeing Alexander again, chagrined to encounter the knight when she was once again so disheveled from a gallop. She tried to brush the feeling aside, chastising herself for her vanity. She gave no heed to what Robert might think about her appearance following their ride, so what reason had she to feel awkward in Alexander's presence? She composed herself and walked over to where the men stood.

"Lord Robert, a pleasant welcome indeed," said Alexander. "Lady Alice, Lady Rosamund, it is a pleasure to see you," he added as the women approached.

"Likewise, Lord Ringewar," replied Rosamund, dropping a curtsy.

"So we meet in the stableyard again," he observed, looking at Rosamund. Despite her surface poise, she was still keenly aware that he encountered her once again pink-faced with her hair escaping into a wild halo around her head. She wondered if it was this aspect of their meeting that he was alluding to, but his expression was perfectly neutral.

Robert laughed. "It is as likely a place as any for my fair cousin, it would seem."

"That was a fine race I saw just now," said Alexander.

Robert gestured expansively at Rosamund. "My cousin here has just proved she is easily my match on horseback," he laughed.

"There was but a handspan in it," she replied generously, a little embarrassed to have beaten her host. "And my horse had a lighter rider, of course." But Robert shook his head, refusing to be mollified.

"The lady affects to defend my honor," winked Robert to Alexander, "but I am duty bound to defend the truth."

Alexander's penetrating gaze brushed over Rosamund. She was acutely aware of the attention.

"I well believe you, Lord Robert. I have seen her riding before."

And now there was no doubt of his meaning. Rosamund blushed and stayed silent. His gaze growing softer at her discomfort, Alexander suddenly broke into a devastating smile.

In that moment Rosamund was quite struck.

She had already acknowledged inwardly that she found him a handsome man, just as her mother had noted. But now, as his usually serious countenance was transformed, she could think of nothing other than that he was the most attractive man she had ever seen. She could not explain it to herself, but as his smile expressed his grudging amusement with her in a way she had not witnessed before, it set aflame feelings for him that she now knew she had harbored since the very first moment she had seen him. She could not take her eyes off him: the lines around his laughing green eyes; the way his smile revealed his white teeth, as straight as his angular jaw; the creases that his smile carved in his sun-browned face. All of it was like some magic concoction that shot straight to her heart and raced through her blood. Had she been standing she would have had to sit down, so breathless did she feel with the sudden realization of her feelings for him.

Alexander noticed her sudden stillness and grew serious once more.

"Do you feel unwell?" he asked with a frown of concern, back to his more sober self. Rosamund recovered herself as best she could.

"No, I am fine, really." She attempted a lighthearted smile but was unable to meet his eyes.

"Some mead for you," declared Robert, making to instruct a servant.

Rosamund shook her head.

"I *am* fine, I assure you," she protested feebly. "Just a little tired after my ride." But she knew she felt anything but tired. Her new awareness of Alexander was singing through her, possessing her mind. Only heaven forbid he become aware of it. How he would laugh if he realized that his liege's young niece, her rank so unequal to his own, had been utterly captivated by him.

She did not know if she convinced either of the men with her explanation, but at that moment she heard footsteps approaching.

"Perhaps Lord Aelward comes," she murmured. They turned to look, Rosamund with relief that Alexander's attention was distracted from her.

It was indeed Lord Aelward, and he and Alexander embraced each other warmly.

"A boon to have you back again so soon," said Lord Aelward.

"The pleasure is all mine," replied Alexander.

"Well, we ought to business," said Lord Aelward to Robert and Alexander.

"Indeed," said Alexander, suddenly looking sterner. "It is time to address the Parnell problem."

Rosamund recalled Lord Aelward's comment on Lord Parnell, their closest neighbor to the north, on the day she had arrived at Duloe, but the men said no more, and as they made to return indoors, Rosamund begged Lord Aelward's pardon to see to any tasks that her aunt or Milicent might need her for. He released her to such a duty, saying, "Bless your diligence, my dear. Yes, run to if you will, and tell your aunt to join us shortly to drink to Lord Ringewar's health before dinner."

Rosamund made her escape, knowing full well she did not deserve her uncle's praise, because he did not know the real reason she had absented herself with such promptness. She had to retreat from the physical presence of Alexander. The strength of the feelings that had washed over her unnerved her, and she could not now have held a sensible conversation with him without the greatest of effort. She was terrified that unless she had some time to gather her thoughts in private he would see straight through her.

Her aunt was in her usual smiling mood when Rosamund arrived in her bower. She had no need of her, and Milicent was absent. "No, my dear," she beamed. "You may make use of your time as you will before we eat." She cast a brief eye over her niece, her gaze resting on Rosamund's mud-spattered dress.

"But pray do change into a clean gown, Rosamund dear."

Rosamund retreated to her bedroom, finding it thankfully unoccupied, and berating herself for how grubby and ungroomed she must have just looked to Alexander's eyes.

A maid had left a bowl of clean water to wash with. She dipped her hands into the cold liquid and rubbed her face with it. Removing the band of linen that had tied back her hair, she took up a wooden comb and smoothed out her tangled mane as best she could before tying it once again. She peered into the bowl of water, which had now stilled, to peruse her reflection. The outline of her hair appeared neat, and in the dim surface of the water she could see no obvious smuts on her face. Her cheeks felt ruddy and refreshed by her wash. She felt a little more composed in contrast to the earlier rush of emotions that had overwhelmed her. Next, she removed her linen day dress and riding hose, leaving her undergarments on for warmth. Opening the room's large wooden cupboard, she hesitated and then took out a blue silk dress. A simple but flattering style, with a gentle flare of the skirt and arms, she dropped it over her head and let the skirt ripple down to her feet. A plain low belt emphasized the flatness of her stomach and the gentle curve of her hips. The generous scoop of the neck revealed the soft, creamy skin of her décolletage. Ordinarily, thought Rosamund, smoothing her dress with her hands, it was unlike her to bother with her appearance overmuch. But it was only right, she thought defensively, to honor her uncle by contributing to a well-presented family for him to preside over. It would atone for her earlier, less elegant appearance. And since her aunt had asked her to change so as to appear more presentable, she was, after all, merely obeying these instructions.

Liar, said Rosamund's conscience, at her pitiful attempts to deceive herself.

CHAPTER FIVE

Once sparked, Rosamund's infatuation with Alexander grew apace. Though she tried to ignore it for days after his return, she could no longer hide from herself that her thoughts were utterly preoccupied with him. When he walked into the same room as her, her heart speeded up a little. When he walked out of the room, it seemed to darken. When she was not in his company, she found her thoughts turning to him, wondering how and where he was spending his time. Did he ever give a thought to her? She doubted it and had to laugh humorlessly at her self-indulgence. But it did not stop her head conjuring up unbidden images of his dark blond head, his compelling face, that heartbreaking smile that had revealed her as forgiven in his eyes.

Unconsciously, she started piecing together a picture of Alexander from the snippets of information dropped in household conversation. She knew that he was unmarried. His bachelor status was not unusual for his age, since many noblemen did not marry until after their third decade. A pity, said the practical side of her nature, for she knew that had he already been bound to another it would have put a quick brake on her fascination for him. As it was, he seemed almost resolutely unattached. Rosamund's heart had given a jump when she had heard this, but she immediately had to quash her pleasure by asking herself why on earth it should matter to her. She had as little chance of being betrothed to an earl's son as to a prince, regardless of whomever else he declined to forge a marital alliance with. And if he did decide in favor of matrimony, there were countless unmarried young noblewomen with a far better claim to such a match, a fact of which she was made continually aware by her aunt and other companions, for one feature that remained a constant from home to home was, of course, gossip. Life for the ladies of the manor consisted of a great deal of it, especially on the matters of marriages and engagements.

At home, Rosamund had often been bored by such chatter; now she found a new fascination in the pastime. She did not do it purposefully, but her mind jumped to attention the instant Alexander's name was mentioned. Like a moth to a flame at these conversations, she would listen in, half ashamed of her curiosity but hating to miss out on any tiny detail about him. She was secretly pleased, as the weeks went by, that there was never a mention of Alexander save for flattering comments. While it was not unusual for a man of his age to still be unmarried, what was more unusual was that Alexander apparently took his knightly vows of chastity more seriously than some. The manor grapevine could not come up with a single instance to prove otherwise, and such stories only added to the esteem in which she increasingly held him. Still, aware he was a handsome man, it struck at Rosamund's heart every time somebody commented on his admirable looks or the needlessness of his single status.

Cautious in her inexperience, she forwent any discussion of her romantic contemplations, even with Maud. Aside from the unrealizable nature of any connection between them, Alexander's very seriousness, his brooding countenance, seemed to discourage her from thinking of her infatuation as a lighthearted amusement to be discussed with others. She also suspected that if Milicent caught scent of her romantic preoccupation, Rosamund would not be spared for a moment from Milicent's malicious amusement.

A fortnight after Alexander's return, a warm balm of fragrant summer air arrived and filled Rosamund with a restless desire to be outside, free of the confines of the house. After completing her usual tasks, she sought out Iolanthe in the bower and begged her permission to take a walk, promising she would take Milicent's children out with her too, ever a good reason to be excused from sitting indoors. She often took them out on excursions — down to play in the stream, run in the meadows, or watch for woodland creatures. After seeing Rosamund's natural affinity with them, Milicent was quite happy for Rosamund to take charge of her offspring. Conversations about the children were among the few times she spoke warmly to Rosamund and, for all Rosamund's personal dislike of Milicent, she could not say that Milicent was an unkind mother.

On this particular morning, Rosamund took the children up the track leading to the new castle. Here, they loved to roll down a stretch of the hill until they were dizzy and then climb back up to repeat the exercise. They were always delighted when Rosamund abandoned grown-up decorum and tumbled with them. She was just picking pieces of grass out of her hair and applauding the children's own acrobatics when she heard the percussion of hoofbeats behind her. Coming down the hill on horseback was a rider wearing a now-familiar blue and gold hauberk: Alexander Ringewar. Her heart gave a little leap. She had seen little of him since the day of his return, save at mealtimes, when he joined the Aelward family down at the manor house. He had stationed himself up at the castle with the rest of the men-at-arms, and most of his day-to-day business was conducted within its imposing stone walls.

Approaching, Alexander reined in his horse. The children, dusting themselves off, were delighted to see the familiar rider and his horse, and they scrambled back up the slope to greet him.

"Take care," warned Rosamund, not wanting them to excite the horse and risk the danger of a kick.

"He'll be fine," assured Alexander, bringing his mount to a disciplined standstill.

"May we pet him, Lord Ringewar?" asked young Robert.

"By all means," replied Alexander. "And

I'm sure he would like a good handful of grass if you could find one."

The children darted off to snatch up handfuls from the edge of the path.

"I commend you for your enthusiasm with the children," said Alexander to Rosamund, his voice good-humored.

Rosamund blushed; he must have seen her tumbling down the hill.

"It reminds me of my own childhood," she said, a little abashed. "They love to play outdoors, and it works off their high spirits. They are an amiable pair."

"Amiable perhaps, but still a handful, I imagine," said Alexander. "On the occasions I have been responsible for them, I have been utterly exhausted by the experience. More tiring than a day's combat."

"But slightly more enjoyable, I hope."

"Naturally. Though keeping control of them certainly required a sharp battle plan."

Rosamund smiled. "I certainly have to keep my wits about me," she concurred. "Palms flat," she added quickly to the children, as they returned with arms outstretched to feed Alexander's amenable steed.

"Quite so," observed Alexander, before inquiring, "Do you walk often?"

"Every day if I can. And taking the children provides further opportunity to do so."

"You are unusual in that, Lady Rosamund. I know many ladies who prefer to stay pale indoors."

"Oh, but there are too many disagreeable days to waste the sunny ones indoors," Rosamund declared.

"I quite agree," said Alexander. "Well, I must to my own duties," he added as his horse finished munching. He waved to the children.

"Be good," he said, then pressed his mount into a walk and proceeded on his way.

Alexander had seen the small party on the hill from quite some distance. He recognized the chestnut hair and slender figure of the comely young woman he had escorted to Duloe. He could have descended on a different route and so avoided Rosamund and her charges, but he found himself inclined to approach and greet her. It was only polite, given her status. As she turned, the breeze blew loose strands of her hair in front of her face, and she had to push them away before she recognized him. She greeted him with an attractive smile. As with the first time he had seen her, he could not help but admire her classic, even features, even as she screwed up her eyes against the sun.

He was pleased to have encountered her away from the stilted setting of the manor house. He also felt somehow pleased at her apparent predilection for the outdoors. He was more familiar with the noble ladies of Court, who did little more than sit around or take gentle strolls around tame castle grounds. He was strangely reluctant to take his leave of the small party. As he looked back over his shoulder, he was suddenly quite taken with the picture of the gamboling threesome in the bright morning sun.

Rosamund returned with the children to the manor house, flushed with secret pleasure as well as her physical exertions. She found the other women in the bower, engaged in a discussion led by Milicent of the notion of courtly love. Maud happily confessed a desire to be the object of a knight's courtly devotion.

"It sounds impossibly romantic," she declared with a sigh.

"Impossible indeed," snorted Iolanthe, when she heard their conversation. "They may pay nothing but lip service to it." It was undoubtedly the case that many instances of courtly love did indeed degenerate into adultery and deceit.

"Well," continued Milicent, "I heard much about it at the royal Court. Why, it was all the rage among the knights there. There was hardly a swain among them who did not talk of his lady for whom he felt such fine love."

It appeared, Milicent recounted, that courtly love was the admiration a knight directed toward an unobtainable lady, often married or his social superior. By the truest account of it, he would dedicate his life in honor of her and love her from afar. There could be an element of flirting and declarations of unremitting love, but the relationship was at heart a chaste one.

"Some knights even swore they had fallen in love with ladies by their reputation of beauty and piety alone, never having met them," Milicent stated.

"Never having met them?" queried Rosamund unbelievingly.

Milicent turned a pained eye upon her.

"Quite so. We are not, after all, talking about *physical* love," she chastised, "but about pure, platonic love, engendered by nobler feelings than base desire."

Rosamund lay in bed that night thinking about courtly love as Milicent had spoken of it, and as her aunt had warned of it. Did knights really swear chaste love for a lady and succeed in conducting themselves accordingly? Had Alexander ever declared such a love for anybody? Gloomily, she supposed that if the lovers did indeed keep their courtship hidden from all other eyes, she would never know of it. He could have promised himself to another a long time ago. Despite herself, she felt a little stab of jealousy in her heart at the thought.

Though it was only late spring, the weather grew unseasonably hot. The manor house was pleasantly cool in the mornings, but the solar was almost too hot by afternoon. As young crops grew taller, village women brought copious amounts of weak ale to the men working in the fields, to quench their thirst. The sun beat down upon the laborers, the heat but a different form of strain to the chafing cold of winter.

Rosamund and Maud retreated to the cool of the forest edge for the walks they had begun taking together, and strolled slowly so as not to get even hotter. On one particular afternoon, they had decided on a path through the westerly forest to avoid the heat, thinking perhaps to splash their feet in the River Lowen before turning back.

At one point, the river opened out into a wide, shallow bed of pebbles, perfect for paddling on a day such as this. It then flowed over a small rocky drop into a deeper, wider pool. A cautious bather could wade among the shallower stones, while those more ambitious could plunge into the deeper water for a full-fledged swim. To bathe in the river's cool water seemed such a luxury in contrast to the wooden tub they would sit shivering in through the winter months on a wash day in the manor house. As Rosamund and Maud approached, they saw the Lowen's bathing pool was deserted. As the river's gentle murmur beckoned, they looked at each other.

"I'd give overmuch for a dip, it's so hot," declared Maud.

"I too," said Rosamund. But the fact was that they had not asked permission to undertake such an activity nor prepared themselves for doing so. They hesitated.

"Oh, I cannot see the harm in it," said Rosamund, throwing decorum to the winds. "We can swim in our underclothes. The sun is so hot we will dry in moments if we rest on the banks a while." The tree canopy was much thinner above the river, allowing the sunshine to play upon the water and the river's edge.

And so Rosamund and Maud undressed to a single layer of undergarments each and waded in. The coolness was delicious. They started off giggling and splashing at their adventure, then swam for a while more quietly. Then, as they were suitably cooled and relaxed by their swim, they climbed out and lay on the smoothest, flattest rocks of the riverbank in the dappled sunlight to rest and let their thin garments dry out.

"Isn't it bliss?" sighed Rosamund a short while later, feeling the twin pleasures of golden heat and the faintest of breezes playing on her skin. "How Lady Aelward will scold us if we come back too pink. But I cannot care."

"Mmmm," was the only reply she got from a soporific Maud.

Squinting at the sun, Rosamund judged that they had another half hour or so before they ought to be returning to the manor house. Just time to take another quick dip and dry off again, she thought. The cool of the water was just too tempting. She left Maud in a contented doze on the bank and decided to take one last dip before they returned. As her long petticoat was nearly dry, she was loath to wet it again, so she slipped it off onto a warm stone. She would be in the water only a few minutes and could not see the harm when it was so unlikely anyone would come by. Dressed only in a thin white sleeveless chemise, she picked her way gracefully to the edge of the water.

Alexander had long been coming to the river to bathe, through his years as page and squire. That afternoon, having finished hawking, he thought he would complete his journey home in the shade of the forest. Having the very same idea as Rosamund and Maud before him, he decided to break his return with a dip to cool him. Listening carefully as he approached, he satisfied himself that there was no female party anywhere close to the bathing pool and strode onward. As he reached the banks of the river, however, he realized his mistake.

Thus it was that, unseen in the shadow of the trees, Alexander caught sight of Rosamund. He could not help but gaze a moment at the feminine figure, undressed further than a man was usually likely to catch sight of, nor ought to, lest it be in his own marriage bed. Rosamund was poised on the edge of the river's deep pool, the sun glinting on her loose hair, wavy where it had dried in the sun, her slender arms above her head, shapely legs first bent, then extended, as she executed a graceful dive into the water. She surfaced just as gracefully, her hair slicked back like an otter's, her skin glistening. With a few practiced strokes she reached the edge of the river again and pulled herself out of the water onto a wide, flat rock, where she sat, looking to Alexander's eyes like some glorious water nymph. Alexander could not help but stare at her beauty. Then he tore his eyes away and melted as quietly as he could back into the forest, Rosamund and Maud still unaware of his presence.

CHAPTER SIX

As Rosamund had predicted, Lady Iolanthe
did indeed chide Rosamund and Maud
when they returned. They did not mention
their swim, which would have exposed them
to yet more of Iolanthe's displeasure over
their lack of modesty. Instead, they let
Iolanthe assume they had merely been dallying in the sunshine. She looked at them
suspiciously.

"Then you'll both be as red as beetroots
tomorrow," she scolded. "What noblewoman wants to look like a serf who has
been working in the fields all day? And did
either of you brush your hair this morning?
If it weren't for your gowns, you'd be
mistaken for peddlers. Now stay in the
shade, my dears, do. And who wouldn't
want to in this weather?"

Despite Iolanthe's warnings, Rosamund
did not think that either of them had caught
a surfeit of sun. The season was early, they

had not bathed for long, and they had lain for the most part where the tree canopy gave a little shade. All the same, she had reason to doubt herself after supper. The family members were all sitting outside, enjoying the gentle rays of the evening sun. Sitting quietly on her wooden chair and gazing out across the gardens, thinking what a pleasant day it had been, Rosamund suddenly had the unmistakeable sense of being watched. Turning, she saw Alexander leaning by one of the apple trees, near to his squire, who sat on the grass. It was Alexander who stared at her. The directness of his gaze held her spellbound for a moment, before he turned away abruptly. *Heavens,* she thought, *I must be looking like a beetroot after all for him to be staring so oddly at me.* She looked up again, determined to shame him into desisting if he were merely amusing himself at the sight of her glowing complexion, but he did not look back. Now, instead, she found herself surreptitiously gazing a little at him: at the strong profile, the dark blond hair turned golden in the sunlight. He looked more relaxed than she had seen him before.

A laugh from the other side of the garden distracted her from her observations. Lord Aelward, the owner of the laugh, strolled over with Robert to the seated group and demanded that a servant be sent to fetch musical instruments.

"To see out the fine evening with some song," he insisted. And so they all gathered together and sang. Rosamund never dared turn back toward Alexander, but she was aware of every note he sang in fine voice behind her.

Alexander had busied himself for much of the day since the incident by the river, but he could not rid himself of the thoughts the scene engendered in him. Something of her grace had called to him, the way she dived into the water so cleanly and boldly, no tentative dipping of toes or squealing at the cold. He was enchanted by the way she had looked so at one with her surroundings on her stone perch, so beautifully at ease in the water. Used to seeing women at court so physically reserved, it was a pleasure to see a woman exhibit mastery of her physical environment and take such joy in it. Her beauty too, was naturally another potent ingredient in the scene that had captured his mind, but here he had to consciously turn his thoughts away from her. He ought not to have seen her at all, and he would not compound the discourtesy, albeit unintentional, by dwelling upon it now. Nonetheless, he found his eyes drawn to her after supper as she sat in the garden in the evening sun, and later as she sang.

It had been several years since Alexander had felt such an attraction to a woman. To all who knew him, he was now a confirmed bachelor. A couple of conjugal matches had been suggested for him, but in both cases the plans had crumbled before he had even met the women in question. The first, an earl's daughter, had become ill and eventually succumbed to a lung complaint. The second potential bride had been fortunate enough to capture the hand of another earl's inheriting son, a position more favorable than Alexander's, and the fledgling plans for his marriage to her had been abandoned. Alexander was not especially disappointed. Now, many years knighted, he was becoming ever more dedicated to this following. Perhaps it was because he had never met a woman who had turned his head enough to tempt him, but he felt no desire to settle down into domestic life. He traveled frequently and could not see how a wife for whom he had little affection, and even less time, would be an advantage to him.

His father disapproved of his failure to take a wife, but since Alexander returned home so infrequently, his father had been little able to exert any influence over him in the matter. In any case, as the earl's second son, there was less obligation upon him to marry and sire an heir quickly. Duloe and the Aelwards had always seemed as much his family as his own, so he experienced no sense of loneliness from choosing not to marry. In contrast, his knightly companions were a source of valued friendship. The camaraderie forged in arms was deep; the sense of loss great when one of his fellow knights fell in battle. It was a harsh life during war but an affirming one for him when at peace. Alexander had dedicated much of his boyhood and his entire adult life to his knighthood, finding in it a sense of purpose and responsibility that matched his serious nature. He could see no higher duty than to serve his liege lord and his king, and to defend his country, with the chivalric code of knights binding him to bravery on the battlefield, loyalty, piety, honesty, chastity, generosity, and to offering protection to any who might need it.

He had first come to Duloe as a young boy of seven to serve as a page in Lord Aelward's home, as was the custom. For the same reasons that daughters spent time as ladies-in-waiting in other noble homes, taking in the son of another nobleman was a gesture of goodwill by a peer and served to strengthen political and social bonds. Twenty-four years on, during which time he had risen to the proud rank of Lord Aelward's chief man-at-arms, Alexander considered Duloe his home almost as much as the place where he had been born. While he loved his family seat of Wickford with a fierce pride, he had given over two decades of his life in service to Duloe. Lord Aelward was like a father to him, and Lady Iolanthe the closest to a mother he had ever had.

After they had finished making music, Rosamund turned to find Alexander standing at her elbow. Lord and Lady Aelward had already risen for a walk around the lawns.

"Would you also care to take a turn?" Alexander asked her.

A small flush crossed Rosamund's cheeks, but she calmed herself. "By all means," she replied evenly with a smile.

They walked without touching, but Rosamund was ever aware of their closeness. If she had extended a hand even a little, she could have touched him. Glancing sideways, she could see the length of his legs as he walked, the brown of his forearm in its rolled-up tunic. Again, his height made her feel slight by comparison. She felt curiously protected by his presence.

"So, does Duloe begin to feel a little like home?" Alexander asked her.

"Oh, I am very happy here," said Rosamund with verve. "I could not have asked for a kinder welcome."

"As I would hope," nodded Alexander in approval. "I would expect nothing less of Lord and Lady Aelward. They have been like family to me for many a year."

"I would be interested to hear more about your own family," Rosamund said. "Your brother is now the earl, I understand. Do you have any other siblings?"

"Sadly not," said Alexander. "My mother died in childbirth with me, and my father did not remarry."

Rosamund was distressed to have launched so abruptly into such a sad history. She could not imagine being without her own mother, to whom she was so close.

"Please forgive me for asking. I had no idea."

"It is quite all right," Alexander replied evenly. "It cannot grieve me too much now, for I never knew her. I would prefer it otherwise, of course, but it is a common enough story. As it is, my brother and his wife reside at Wickford now, since my father died and my brother inherited."

"And how long is it since your brother inherited?"

"Three years." Alexander frowned. Seeing this, Rosamund imagined that he must have forged a stronger bond with his surviving parent and had felt the loss more keenly.

"Were you close to your father?" she asked kindly. Perhaps it was a more personal question than she ought to have asked, yet once again something about Alexander had elicited directness in her.

Alexander's face darkened again and there was a pause before he spoke.

"My father made it clear to me over the years that he blamed me for my mother's death. Our relationship was never a happy one. But I must concede some sympathy for his view; I believe he loved my mother very much."

"But you were just an infant. It could not possibly be considered your fault," protested Rosamund, with a rush of empathy for such a tiny child's predicament.

"No," Alexander acknowledged. "Yet, it is the case that my father allowed my mother's death to sour the relationship between him and me from the first."

"I am most sorry for you that he did," said

Rosamund. "It seems most unfair to you."

Alexander sighed. "Well, perhaps he did not blame me entirely, but it cannot be easy to have one person exchanged for another in such a stark fashion; hard for a new love to flourish in the wake of an older one lost so suddenly."

Alexander was surprised by his own words. He had not talked of his mother's death nor his unhappy relationship with his father in years, and then only to his brother. He could hardly remember expounding upon such a theory before about his relationship with his father. Rosamund was in fact the first person in many years to actually ask him about such things. Were she from a slightly higher social stratum, or a generation older, she would have known his family history better and not needed to ask. Yet, curiously for someone who spoke little about his feelings, it felt strangely natural to expand upon her questions. Something about her was drawing him out, perhaps her air of genuine concern. He had always found those with an unfeigned interest in others to be a higher caliber of acquaintance than those within whom self-interest reigned. He found he wanted to talk to Rosamund. Though he had not acknowledged it consciously before this moment, he knew he had not ended up at her side after the music by accident.

"I daresay, for yes, death is a shocking circumstance no matter how aware we are of the possibility beforehand," Rosamund was saying, feeling a rush of affection now for Alexander, wanting to defend him belatedly from his father's antipathy toward him.

"I hope at least he was proud of your accomplishments as a knight," she continued.

"I regret to say he considered it a waste of time to train me as a knight, but it is the fashion of the time, and he acceded to it."

Rosamund clasped her hands together in her awkwardness. "I must apologize again. I have elicited too many unhappy memories on such a fine evening." The sun was sinking now, bathing them with its final rosy glow.

"Not at all," said Alexander. His face softened a little as he looked to her, her hair glowing copper in the light, her brow furrowed, no doubt in consternation at the way the conversation had gone.

"It is in the past now," he said in gentle tones, "and I had many years in which to come to terms with my father's opinion of me. It is not now an opinion which I even have to bear anymore, though I mean no disrespect to my father's passing. Normally

I would not even speak of these things. But I find you have gained my confidence with ease, Lady Rosamund." He paused on the path, forcing her to stop too, lest she leave him behind. Rosamund could tell Alexander was looking at her, but suddenly she could not return his gaze. The very nearness of him made her heart beat faster. In so close an encounter, surely, he couldn't fail to see the emotion he stirred in her if she raised her eyes to his. She didn't know how to reply. Looking about her, she saw Lord and Lady Aelward had gone out of sight around the corner of the house.

"We should continue. The sun is nearly gone."

Alexander inclined his head. "As you wish."

On her return to the house, Rosamund was swept away by Iolanthe to help ready her for bed. She was brushing her aunt's hair when Iolanthe spoke up.

"I saw you having a pleasant turn about the garden with Lord Ringewar," she said. "Which reminded me to speak with you. I have not forgotten that your uncle and I are quitted with the task of helping to find you a husband. We have yet but mentioned it since you came, but we will not be neglectful in our duty." She turned briefly to beam at Rosamund in what she must have thought a reassuring manner.

"Of course, I know you will be aware that Lord Ringewar — apart from not being the marrying kind, which is quite the most frustrating thing for many noblewomen I know, I can tell you — is a little above your rank, no need to tell you that. But there will be opportunity enough for us to help you in your own marriage plans during your stay."

Rosamund's first reaction was one of relief. Iolanthe's tone was certainly not one of a woman who had conceived of Rosamund's feelings for Alexander. Presumably the sight of Rosamund walking with him had merely reminded Iolanthe to have such a conversation with Rosamund. But Rosamund's second reaction was more morose. To have the inferiority of her connections acknowledged out loud poured cold water over the idling fantasies that had been playing in her mind ever since she realized she harbored feelings for Alexander. She knew that her aunt spoke the truth, yet lingering in the back of her mind had been Iolanthe's own fortune in marriage, a spark of hope that Rosamund now realized she had unwittingly been entertaining.

Iolanthe had married well when she had

captured the hand of Aelfric Aelward, the young third Earl of Duloe, thirty years previously. She and her sister, Rosamund's mother, were the daughters of a baron who had shown great loyalty to King Henry during his reign. As a reward, the king had seen to it that the baron's eldest daughter, Iolanthe, married advantageously. Rosamund was aware of the serendipity of Iolanthe's climb in rank. But her own story held no parallel. There was no pressure on Alexander to marry below him; no reason for Rosamund to be plucked from the lower ranks of nobility as her aunt had been. Rosamund forced herself to smile pleasantly at her aunt's words.

"Thank you for thinking to speak to me," she said. "But if truth be told, Lady Aelward, I have not thought of marriage at all since my arrival. Besides," she continued brightly, as she continued to brush Iolanthe's loose tresses, "you have all made me so welcome since I arrived that I have no desire to leave." That much, at least, was the truth.

"Why, my dear," laughed Iolanthe. "I don't know a girl alive who doesn't put thought to whom she might marry. We have been keeping you too busy if you have not had time to do so. But I am relieved if you aren't fretting too much about the matter."

Rosamund went to bed that night with conflicting thoughts. If she were sensible about it, Rosamund knew, she should bury her feelings for Alexander until they faded, given that there was no chance of any union resulting from her attraction to him. He was of considerably higher rank than her, and if he did marry, it would undoubtedly eventually be to a noblewoman of similar standing and fortune to his own.

Yet now an insight into his life had only drawn her closer to him. She wondered how it must have felt for Alexander, always unfavored by his father, never able to redeem himself in his father's eyes, and no chance at all of that redemption once his father passed on. Was that why he put so much store by his knightly duty? Was he still attempting to show that his father had been wrong to judge him unworthy of being a knight? She wondered if at his father's death he might have felt relief at the dissolution of the conflict between them, or whether it had left him still trying to please the ghost of a man who would now never acknowledge his son's worth.

CHAPTER SEVEN

On the occasions when they did not join the ladies in the evening, Lord Aelward, Lord Robert, and Alexander were witnessed engaged in regular somber meetings, tucked away in Lord Aelward's study or pacing the grounds together, heads bent low, their expressions grave. More frequently than usual, messengers on horseback were sent and received at the castle. Rosamund would see her aunt looking at her menfolk in concern, but Iolanthe refused to reveal her own thoughts on the matter.

Despite the serious mood that encompassed the noblemen, the next public proclamation Lord Aelward made was on a most cheerful note, as he ordered the traditional May feast to be held. All the manor was invited to make merry, from Lord Aelward himself down to the humblest servants and villeins.

As a hot sun sank once again into a

beautiful evening, fires were lit on the grounds of the manor house and lanterns hammered into the ground. Four large boars had been roasting on spits for some hours, and the Great Hall tables overflowed with tempting fare. The manor house servants were obliged to be fit enough to see to their tasks, but as long as they could do so and remain standing, a blind eye would be turned to the quantity of ale and wine they might consume.

Rosamund prepared her toilet for the evening with a little extra care. She knew the men-at-arms would come down the hill and join them for the evening. Frequently, she had been left feeling restless and dissatisfied each night when she departed the solar and Alexander's presence: she found herself edgy with anticipation to see him again the next day and plunged into disappointment if he was engaged by some other matter. So tonight, she could not help her thoughts turning to him again, how he might tarry a little in the lamplight after the feasting and perhaps linger for longer near her as they sang and danced.

The feasting began at seven o'clock. Musicians in the Great Hall's gallery struck up with jolly tunes; they would play through the night. Large kegs of ale were stationed on wooden trestles and provided a constant stream of refreshment for the cups and tankards of anyone who cared to turn the tap. Villagers swarmed up the hill to join the feast; there were not enough seats for all in the Great Hall, so a merry throng grew outside. There was a hubbub of shouting, singing, and laughter. Musicians from the village were already playing their fiddles to rival the music within the Great Hall, and those who had eaten their fill, for the time being at least, were already starting up the dancing.

Maud and Rosamund sat next to each other on the dais, enjoying the copious fare of the feast, listening to the musicians, and tapping their feet in time. Eventually, when their appetites were sated, they excused themselves and made from the Great Hall into the courtyard outside, where more merrymaking was now in full flow under the stars. It was a warm night, perfect for such an event. Little though Maud knew, Rosamund was secretly hoping that in the moving throng of revelers she might wend her way into the path of Alexander. Anticipation fluttered in her stomach at the thought. She had not seen him in the hall and wondered if he had eaten outside or, indeed, had not yet come.

Everywhere Rosamund looked there was raucous conviviality afoot. Scullions made merry with footmen; the young ladies made eyes at the squires. On a bench by a fire, Lord Aelward was drinking with the best of the village men, rollicking laughter emanating from him as loudly as from the rest of them. She smiled as she watched him briefly, for the riotous atmosphere was infectious. She and Maud beamed at each other in unspoken agreement and headed to join the throng of dancers.

Two dances later, Rosamund felt a thirst. She voiced her desire to Maud, who would have joined her, but at that moment a young squire stepped in and asked Maud if he might partner her instead. Rosamund cheerfully acceded and waved Maud happily away as she was whirled off back into the dance.

Looking about, Rosamund tapped the arm of a serving boy, asking him to bring her a glass of wine. With her aunt's prior permission, Rosamund saw no reason not to partake of a small taste. After a minute or so she turned around to see if she could see the servant returning with her wine. Instead, with a thrill of recognition, she saw Alexander approaching, his tall frame attracting her attention immediately. He was holding a glass of ale, and when he saw her he nodded and, to her nervous delight, came over.

"Lady Rosamund. Are you enjoying the feast?" he asked of her, his green eyes looking almost amber as they blazed the reflection of the fires.

"Very much," she enthused.

"Would you allow me to fetch you a drink?" he said, noting her empty hands.

"I have already asked for one — in fact, here it is now." With thanks, she accepted the glass proffered and took a sip.

"It makes a change, does it not, to our usual evening routine?" Alexander asked, gazing around at the scene. Two young squires were sporting with a bucket of water several yards away, and some village girls close by shrieked with laughter as they were splashed.

"It is a little louder than the usual entertainment," agreed Rosamund.

As she spoke, some rambunctious young village men caroused past them and bumped into her. In quick courtesy, Alexander's hand shadowed Rosamund's elbow for fear she would be knocked off balance. Thanking him, she saw a frown cross his face at the men's actions, which remained as he surveyed the scene.

"There will be a good deal of such tom-foolery this eve," he said. There it was, thought Rosamund, the sober note of disapproval she feared he had once applied to her so early in their acquaintance.

"They work hard," said Rosamund in conciliatory fashion. "We cannot begrudge them an evening of indulgence."

He shook his head, as if to dispel his somber mood. "But doubtless you are right, Lady Rosamund. With luck, the most we will be faced with tonight are those who imbibe so much ale they fall over and make themselves ill. I speak of the women as well as the men."

Rosamund laughed. "I wonder if I should put my glass away for fear of incurring your disapproval," she teased.

"You will brook no disapproval from me tonight," said Alexander. "I accede to your thoughts on the matter. And I am known to have made freely with the wine myself in my younger days. But come," he said, suddenly. "Would you care to take a stroll over to the rose garden where it is a little quieter?"

Anywhere in your company, Rosamund thought happily, but she merely inclined her head in polite acceptance. After only a few sips of her wine she had already begun to feel deliciously light-headed.

"So, do you not rest from the burden of your responsibilities anymore?" Rosamund asked, half serious but also with a teasing glance to his tankard of ale.

"I make allowances for youth and high spirits," he said, slightly more serious again. "I would not be much of a chief at arms if I did not. The men must have their fun. But I have sworn to perform my chivalric duty to the best of my ability, and I have learned from experience that I serve it better if I exercise temperance, even on such occasions."

Rosamund would have thought the words pompous spoken by another man, but the light in his eyes had her believing he meant every word. It was as others had said: Alexander Ringewar seemed the most dedicated of men to his knightly calling.

"And how fare you here, Rosamund?" he suddenly asked her. "Does life at Duloe suit you still?"

She noticed how he had not called her by her title, just her given name. The way he said it gave her a shiver of pleasure.

"Yes, as I have said before, I am most happy here. I do not want for company, and I am kept busy in my tasks." She wished she could tell him that it was his own presence that brightened her days the most of all. "And I have perfected the art of embroidery nearly as much as I can stand," she added sardonically, wondering if the wine already worked to undermine her discretion.

Alexander laughed. "I don't imagine a woman such as you would be much satisfied by a life of embroidery."

A woman such as her. What kind of woman *did* he think of her as, she wondered. It pleased her a little that he had taken the time to form any opinion of her at all. She could only hope it was not an uncomplimentary one. It did not sound so.

"What else do you do with your days, Rosamund Galleia?" Alexander asked.

She shrugged her shoulders.

"I talk with the other women. We entertain one another with music and singing. I also learn languages, for my uncle has been kind enough to allow the chaplain to tutor me. Sometimes Lord Robert takes it upon himself to teach me some history. And when I have the chance, I like to read."

"You have been taught? I have always thought it a little unjust that all noblewomen were not taught to read and write as a matter of course," mused Alexander. "Lady Aelward is of course fortunate enough to have learned to read. She would read Latin verse to me to school me when I was young and, while I did not understand all of it, the sound of her voice was always soothing. I remember it fondly." He paused in recollection. "Yet, it is rare for women to be taught to such an extent, and I know not why. Many women have the intelligence for it. I am sure of it."

"I daresay men for the most part do not need us to read," said Rosamund, "and I suspect some of them do not want us to, either. A woman who can read can educate herself. A woman who cannot knows only what she is told."

"A cynical view." Alexander looked at her thoughtfully, and Rosamund wondered if she had said too much. What was it about him that unconsciously urged her to say more than she intended to? "But I can imagine instances where that would be true," he added, to her relief. "But what has led you to this opinion, Lady Rosamund?"

"I have heard it said within my presence," said Rosamund. "By noblemen visiting my father's home. They did not seem to care for a woman with ideas above her station in life and were happy to say so."

"So tell me, what have you gathered that men do want of their noblewomen?" Alexander inquired of her. She could not tell if he were mocking her a little, for surely he would know the answer himself, but she would give him a straightforward reply.

"Why, a good and obedient wife who will provide him with sons and heirs," she replied. "A competent lady of the manor to manage his household, and perhaps a little company in the evenings if he does not always prefer the company of other men. And perhaps an attractive adornment on his arm, such that other men might look upon his choice of wife with approval."

Alexander gave a cough of laughter.

"I detect a note of world-weariness again there, fair Rosamund," he said. "But let me ask you. Is it so wrong for a man to want a beautiful wife?"

Something in the way he asked the question made the butterflies dart in her stomach again.

"I suppose it is only natural," she conceded.

"Natural, but you disapprove?"

She attempted to express herself more fully. "I would be foolish if I disapproved of an attraction between a man and a woman, if that is what you are referring to. That is not what I mean. I am concerned more with when a woman is desired only for what she looks like, only for her wealth — when she is not cherished for who she is in any way, only for what she can give a man."

"And what if she gives happiness to a man? Would that not be a goodly thing to give?" Alexander's voice was searching.

"I would deny nobody a union that brought happiness," replied Rosamund. "I talk of tangible possessions: wealth, alliances, position. And when beauty has a woman treated as a bauble."

"You speak with spirit on the matter." Alexander glanced at her with an amused smile. "Your ambitions are noble, and I am not disagreeing with them, but am I hearing the voice of a romantic? Would you have us all marry for love?"

"Yes," she said forcefully, then shook her head, embarrassed. He would think her a naïve fool.

"I mean I wish that I could be a romantic, but I am aware of the purposes of marriage and the purpose that women serve within it. I do not imagine it all to be done away with, for us to be free to marry whomever we choose. There is no choice for us other than to play out our part in the plan men design for us."

"And now you sound distinctly jaded again." Alexander frowned. "Do you think all men are happy with this arrangement?"

Rosamund hesitated; his question made her pause for thought.

"I could not say," she conceded.

"Young men are also persuaded into marriages," said Alexander. "Marriages that they would not have chosen if it were a decision of the heart. It is not outside of their experience to want to marry for love and have it denied them."

Rosamund could not disagree when he put it like that.

"I must acknowledge it," she admitted. "I confess my opinion on the matter naturally comes of closer consideration of a woman's position." She hesitated, then continued.

"But a woman has no power within a marriage. A man may do as he likes with his wife, chosen with love or not. She is chattel and is expected to do his bidding."

Alexander nodded.

"I grant you that in return," he said. "It is a feature of a wife's existence that she is inferior in status to her husband. I am not sure how it would run were there to be none in charge, though I am sure it will displease you for me to favor the arrangement." He paused. "But you would be surprised, within the confines of the marital home, how the supposedly inferior party may exercise her power. Why, I have seen it here at Duloe on many an occasion. I refer of course to your uncle and aunt. Does your aunt have no sway over her husband?" His eyes twinkled a little at her. Rosamund had to laugh, and he joined in.

"You are right in this instance, of course," she acceded, still smiling. "My aunt will have it her way on many occasions. My uncle humors her most indulgently. There is a strong affection between them. I envy it."

"You envy it?" Alexander picked up on her comment. "You do not yet have cause to envy. No unkind man has captured you in marriage."

She corrected herself. "It was a hasty remark. I meant only that when I am to marry, I hope I should be as fortunate in the character of my husband as my aunt is in hers."

Alexander's voice was soft. "I find it hard to imagine you with a husband who will not care for you." He was looking at her now, his expression grown more serious again.

Rosamund replied swiftly. "But who is to say? To me, it is the luck of a coin toss as to whether I will have a kind husband or a cruel one. I will not be the one to decide. I will merely be expected to be grateful for a suitable proposal." She returned to her point. "My aunt has been fortunate to marry a man who cares for her and looks after her well, but not all women are so lucky. Some have husbands who not only do not care for them, but who enjoy their power over them and abuse it unmercifully."

"I cannot deny it," said Alexander. She heard him sigh. "But do not be too down-hearted, Rosamund. Would you not trust your father or your uncle to propose a reasonable husband for you? Do you think they will not consider his character even a little?"

"It is a fair question," she acknowledged after a pause. "I would indeed hope they would not choose someone whom they knew to be a cruel man. But they will not know him well. They are unlikely to know how he comports himself in the privacy of his own home. It will be for me to find that out, and I will already be his wife."

Alexander looked at her intently, and it unsettled her. He had been kind, easier to talk to this past quarter hour than she could have imagined. She shook her head.

"I have spoken too much. You will think me ungracious. I am not unaware of the privileges of my position, nor the kindness of my family. I know I have much to be grateful for."

Alexander spoke softly again. "I do not think you ungracious, Rosamund. You are not afraid to voice your opinions, and with feeling. I find it refreshing."

Rosamund was not unpleased by his compliment, but she shook her head again. He seemed not entirely unsympathetic to her thoughts, but of course she should remember that a truly courteous knight would doubtless not wish to offend a lady by disagreeing with her outright. Perhaps he was merely humoring her.

"You listened indulgently, or I would not have spoken so forcefully or so long," she said. "You have been most forbearing with me. Many would not hear it so politely, and I would not speak it."

"But I am glad you did."

Rosamund glanced up at Alexander. She could not fathom the expression with which he beheld her.

Maud suddenly appeared at Rosamund's shoulder.

"You cannot languish here in the dusk any longer. Come and dance, both of you!" she entreated, pulling at Rosamund's sleeves. "I thought you were stopping but to quench your thirst, Rosamund." Laughingly, Rosamund let Maud take her hand.

"If it pleases you," she said.

"And you too, Lord Ringewar?" said Maud to Alexander, blithely unaware of how self-conscious Rosamund would have been at asking him the very same question.

He smiled but shook his head regretfully, gesturing at the tankard in his hand. "Perhaps a little later."

Rosamund felt a little wrench at his decline.

"Do you not dance?" she inquired, not quite willing to let him go so easily.

He gave an apologetic smile. "I must find your uncle next. I need to speak with him before the hour gets any later."

Hiding her reluctance, Rosamund allowed Maud to lead her away to the courtyard, where the fiddlers were in full swing.

An hour later and shiny-faced with exertion, Rosamund excused herself once again from the dancing and took herself off to rest on a settle. As she sat, the minutes ticking by, she felt the bubble of euphoria which had buoyed her up all day begin to subside. She had danced a good while, and now she had sat a little while too. Alexander knew where she was, but he had clearly found a more pressing engagement elsewhere. Her mood sank further. She felt wretched at how much the thought of seeing him filled her with a thrill of excitement and how that thrill dissipated in his absence. Suddenly no longer in the mood for dancing, she glanced at a candle. It was gone eleven, and the first stirrings of tiredness brushed at her. She knew if she stayed up longer it would be for the sole purpose of seeing Alexander again. A small grain of pride welled up in her. She refused to tarry for that single reason. If Alexander did not wish to seek her company that was his choice, but she would not sit and mope as it became ever more obvious that he was not returning. Disconsolate, she headed resolutely for her bedchamber.

She sat on her bed and tried to put the feeling aside before loosing her hair, undressing, blowing out the candles, and lying down. Maud was still not back. The sounds of revelry filtered in through the narrow windows. She wished she had seen Alexander again, wished she remained more lighthearted when they had spoken; wished he had danced with her, something she now realized she had been hoping for all day. The promise of such an occurrence had faded with his disappearance and vanished with her own departure. For her, the day's festivities were over.

CHAPTER EIGHT

When Rosamund awoke in the morning, Maud was lying asleep in the next bed, her blond curls tumbling messily over her pillow. Godith appeared to have arisen already. Maud woke when Rosamund started to wash and dress.

"So, sleepyhead," teased Rosamund, trying to seem her usual self. "What time did you come to bed? I did not hear you."

Maud screwed up her face against the sunshine, propped herself up on one elbow, and gave a guilty grimace. "It was some way after twelve. And I confess it might have been later, except that Lady Iolanthe came to shepherd me in. But guess! Sir Philip asked me to dance. Three times! I was in heaven and quite forgot the time. What a wonderful night!" She sank back against her pillow, reminiscing. "And you?" she inquired. "I saw you not after I last went to dance."

"I was to bed by eleven," Rosamund admitted.

"And missed so much revelry?" Maud looked disapproving.

"I started to tire," said Rosamund. She could not admit it was her disappointment with Alexander's absence that had prompted her retreat to bed.

Later that morning, after breakfast, Rosamund took her despondent spirits down to the domain of Brunhilde's kitchens by request of Iolanthe, who had asked her to familiarize herself with the planning of the meals for the coming week.

Rosamund was sitting at the large wooden table observing the cooks calculating the vegetables and game needed for the next few days when the most senior chambermaid whisked in.

"Where is that chit Marie?" she tutted. "She is supposed to be helping me with the bedding, and I cannot find her anywhere."

"Marie is indisposed," Brunhilde informed her in a knowing tone of voice. "I saw her first thing," she continued, returning to the scoring of some ham, "getting some water at the well to soothe her head. She claims she is the worse for her indulgences, and so I believe her. Though I suspect a better story of her tiredness." She paused while the chambermaid and others present hovered, hoping for further enlightenment.

"Now what better story would that be?" said the chambermaid.

"Well," said Brunhilde, not averse to continuing her theory. "I saw that she spent most of the evening dallying around the fireside in the small courtyard for quite some time with Lord Ringewar, as some of you will have seen too. Most friendly they seemed, if you catch my meaning. Anyhow, around ten o' the clock he was nowhere to be found, and she had disappeared too. Now I oughtn't to cast aspersions, but it's a shocking thing what ale will encourage people to do on these occasions." She giggled lasciviously, and the others all joined in. Recovering herself slightly, Brunhilde noted Rosamund's still face. Leaning across, she patted her arm good-humoredly.

"My dear, you must forgive an old woman her gossip. But it is the way of the world. People will have their fun." And with that, the servants all set to a keen discussion on the known events of the previous night.

Until that moment in the kitchen, Rosamund's infatuation with Alexander had been nothing but a pleasurable ache. At Brunhilde's words she felt an unpleasant twist in her stomach. Her world turned darker. An image came unbidden into her head of Alexander and Marie in an embrace, his handsome face leaning toward her vivacious one in the evening firelight. She felt a little sick. *What about his vows?* she thought to herself. *Honor? Chivalry?* It was all a lie, and she had believed it. But she knew she was not simply outraged at his hypocrisy. No, she had no doubt about what emotion had just overcome her. Jealousy, and a spring tide of it. No matter that Alexander ought not to be her concern. No matter that his knightly conduct was not of the temperance he had claimed it to be. In the deepest part of her heart, she could not stem the surge of jealousy at hearing how the object of her affections had bestowed his own affections upon another.

So when she had been hoping he would return to the dancing, Rosamund thought bitterly, he was in fact sporting with Marie in flickering firelight and hidden corner. She had never stood a chance of capturing his attention again last night. Inwardly, she chastised herself for talking so seriously at the feast. No wonder he had turned to Marie after she had bored him in the rose garden. What man wanted to talk about the social position of women in the midst of a celebration, especially a man who had risked repeated injury and death in the defense of man and woman alike? Alexander had been attentive enough, but doubtless she had mistaken his politeness for interest. She sat like stone at the table, surrounded by laughter, as she affected an indifferent smile.

That evening she saw Alexander again as he arrived to eat at the manor house. With the extent of her infatuation revealed to her, she could barely look at him. Yet when she did, it almost stopped her heart. As she looked surreptitiously out of the solar window, she knew she was still fascinated by everything about him: the strength in his hands as he brought his horse to a standstill, the way he threw himself confidently off his horse and tossed the reins to a groom with a nod of thanks, the way he stood, the confidence in his walk, the line of his profile, the sound of his voice. Everything masculine in his countenance and build, yet everything courteous in his manner: it seemed a combination destined to defeat her resolve to dismiss him from her affections.

Alexander ate with the healthy appetite of a man with a clear conscience, Rosamund observed. She could also see Marie standing at the far end of the hall. She studied the girl more intently than she ought to have, but Marie did not give herself away with any lingering glances toward the dais. The girl looked a little tired, but no obvious pallor of guilt hung over her. Still, Rosamund knew how she hid her own feelings for Alexander every day so that even Maud, seemingly, did not suspect anything. Small wonder the chaplain looked at them all so often with an almost habitual disapproval.

Iolanthe noticed Rosamund was hardly eating.

"I do hope it is not from too much excitement last night my dear," she chided. "Or perhaps you are still tired. Eat up either way, dearie. I cannot have you fading away."

Rosamund was grateful for her aunt's concern. After Alexander's unwitting rejection, she was glad at that moment that someone at Duloe showed a care for her.

The weather had stayed fine since the feast, and after their meal the family filed out of the Great Hall into the adjoining antechamber, thence to make their way outside for their customary evening air. Shafts of evening sunshine penetrated the room; the wooden shutters had been opened to let in the warm air.

"We must talk again," frowned Lord Aelward to Alexander, who followed him, "but I must see to getting a message written and sent to London directly, if you could spare me a quarter hour to do so." His eye rested for a moment on Rosamund, who hovered glumly by a wooden settle, and he brightened.

"Perhaps you would care to take Rosamund for a turn around the gardens before returning, Alexander."

Alexander inclined his head. "My pleasure," he replied amiably.

Just words, thought Rosamund savagely, thinking once again of with whom his pleasure really lay. Despite herself, she still felt an unhappy little flurry of butterflies in her stomach as he approached her. She wished she could stop responding in such a way when she saw him. She could only hope she presented a picture of unruffled dignity as he gestured the way and followed her outside.

On the customary evening sojourns in the garden, Rosamund usually took the time to appreciate at leisure the house's impressive stonework, its thick oak doors with their ironwork, the thin, graceful arches of the first-floor windows, with their matching oak and iron shutters. On this evening, however, she was too busy fuming from Alexander's unintentional rejection of her the night before.

Alexander was quiet, still suffering the effects of ale perhaps, she thought caustically, or, more likely, fatigued from his nocturnal adventures. He answered her conversational attempts in monosyllables for the most part.

Eventually Rosamund, hardly in a mood to converse with him to begin with, almost snapped at him.

"I must apologize if I bore you."

He started in surprise. "Not at all. I am more than interested in what you were saying."

"That remains to be seen, for you are leaving the distinct impression that you are not, for you have hardly spoken a word to me in return."

"I was not aware of my neglect. I must apologize. I intend only courtesy."

"You may intend only courtesy, but your lack of interest was clear in your tone and your countenance." Her anger was clear in her voice.

"You must forgive me. I am a little distracted this evening."

Really, thought Rosamund sarcastically. *He neglects to say why, but I know the very reason.* But she didn't say it. Instead she retorted sharply, "So it would seem." She knew she was being harsh, but she couldn't help herself.

Alexander's face showed his surprise at her sudden outburst of bad temper.

"I can only apologize again. I can assure you I have never found your conversation to be either trifling or boring."

I disagree, Rosamund wanted to shout at him. *Is that not why you chose to indulge in horseplay with a serving girl instead of conversing further or dancing with me at the feast?*

"Rosamund," he said with quiet concern, "you seem angry with me for more than simply a little distraction on my part."

Rosamund was mortified at his insight. She had thought him almost entirely insensible of her. She could not answer him, could not tell him that she was angry because of the unwanted emotions he engendered in her. In the absence of a response from her, Alexander continued.

"I did not mean to insult you by my neglect of you just now. I must reiterate: my mind has been on other matters this past day or so."

"Then perhaps I should inconvenience you no further," snapped Rosamund, unable to temper her reply. "Pray proceed with your thoughts." With this, she quickened her pace and marched off across the grass, leaving a surprised Alexander in her wake.

In the house later, Rosamund knew she had sought out a disagreeable conversation with him on purpose, and a wave of shame overcame her at her petulant behavior. A little voice reminded her that even if his distraction *was* caused by Marie, it was actually none of her concern. But she was aware that her bruised heart had been searching to strike out and hurt in return, for it had suddenly seemed too hard to endure her misery with any grace.

CHAPTER NINE

As an earl, Lord Aelward was exceeded only in rank by the dukes and marquesses of the land and the king himself. Being of higher rank and wealthier than Rosamund's father, he owned more land and supported a household more than twice the size of Baron Galleia's. With an unhappy prescience of uncertain times ahead, when King Stephen had acquired the throne several years earlier, Lord Aelward had started the project of building Duloe Castle. It was one of only a fraction of such new and imposing stone edifices whose construction actually had the permission of the king. Lord Aelward had considered the burden of the project a wise investment in the future protection of his manor, and it would seem he was to be proved right.

In the last few months his closest neighbor, Lord Parnell, had continued to refuse to commit himself publicly to the support of King Stephen, which was tantamount to declaring himself a supporter of Matilda. In outright defiance of the king, Lord Aelward was aware, Parnell had been building fortifications on his land for several years without royal permission, and he had recently appropriated land belonging to a neighboring baron loyal to Stephen. If all this were not cause enough for Lord Aelward to be wary of his neighbor's intentions, last week news had come from the village that Parnell's men-at-arms had attacked a village on the same neighboring baron's land. Seeing the baron's small military force routed by Lord Parnell's men, the villagers had fled for their lives into the forest, thence to find shelter in villages further afield. A few sorry souls from the exodus had made their way to Duloe to tell the story.

Lord Aelward had sent a messenger to Parnell a fortnight ago, demanding an end to his aggression. Now Lord Aelward sat at his desk, his face grave, Alexander and Robert facing him in high-backed wooden chairs.

"Several nights ago, the village of Hasthwaite was razed to the ground and its supplies stolen. The villagers fled into the woods and were found wandering in the forest scavenging for food. They have no homes to return to. We must assume this is Lord Parnell's answer to our request. As you know, Hasthwaite belongs to Baron de Mowbray and borders my own land." Lord Aelward scowled, then continued to his conclusion.

"You know I am not a war-hungry man, but Parnell's actions are too close for comfort and now threaten lives. We must see that this is stopped. There is nothing for it. We must raise arms and answer him. We go to battle."

No sooner had Lord Aelward made his announcement public than the atmosphere in the castle changed. A heavy sense of foreboding fell over the inhabitants. The smithy fires burned night and day making horseshoes, arrowheads, and blades for sword and axe. The armorers did not stop work until every man was fitted out with battle attire suited to his station. The constable was seen ceaselessly drilling the men-at-arms, while the knights in their turn instructed the drafted village men in the actions expected of them during battle.

Rosamund was deeply distressed on behalf of the villagers of the neighboring manors upon hearing their homes and crops had been destroyed, and yet more so for those who had lost their lives.

"Yet must there be battle?" Rosamund asked desperately of her aunt.

"My dear, it pains me to say it, but there is no other choice. Our neighbor is attacking the villages in between his and our lands. Next it may be our own. And your uncle will never stand for murder on his land, and a better man he is that he acts on behalf of those who are already being attacked, for whom he has no manorial responsibility. Nay, Lord Parnell needs to be stopped. If he is not stopped ten miles from here, it may be here on our doorstep that we challenge him next. Your uncle has no choice. Battle it must be."

Lord Aelward's decision thus played an unwitting role in swiftly curing Rosamund of her self-pitying mood. As the days had passed after the feast, Rosamund had chastised herself for her unseemly conduct toward Alexander. She had noted miserably that since her last exchange with him, he had spent less time at the manor house. And while Rosamund could be fairly sure that any dalliance between Alexander and Marie was unlikely to take a more serious turn — Marie was a servant girl after all, and Alexander was hardly going to pursue an engagement with her — still the occasional sight of the girl did not assuage Rosamund's jealousy.

Her heart had given a little bump when Lord Aelward had made his pronouncement, and she felt herself put to shame by her trivial romantic preoccupations. When Alexander had referred to being distracted during their conversation the other night, perhaps he had been referring to this. And instead of being understanding, she had berated him. She wanted an opportunity to apologize to him but, painful though his presence was to her, he was still little to be found at the manor house. At least, she thought, it explained his absence since her outburst.

She was disturbed at the thought of Alexander going into battle. She knew that he had faced such fighting before and was an experienced warrior. But she also knew that a single arrow could end the career and life of even the most skillful knight. She wanted no harm to come to him even though she had no claim to him whatsoever. The thought of never seeing him again filled her with dread. *How had this happened?* she asked herself. How had she fallen in love with a man who was legions above her in social rank, who expressed no interest in marriage but instead likely indulged in base romantic entanglements that directly contradicted one of the knightly vows he supposedly held so dear? Whose only encouraging action toward her romantically was the condescension to break into a laugh or a smile on the rarest of occasions? Was it because he was so unattainable that she had let herself foster such an attraction to him? She wished it were so, but she suspected that no matter the situation, that golden head and brooding presence would have captured her heart regardless.

When the men departed for battle, the women and village folk left behind would be more vulnerable. It was not unheard of for an attack to be made on the manor from which an opposing army had been raised. Thus, while Lord Aelward and Alexander were marshaling their military forces, Lady Aelward was in charge of the hive of activity entailed in moving her household up the castle hill. Ordinarily, she might have conducted the move in a whirlwind of fuss and furor, reflected Rosamund with affection for her aunt, but the seriousness of the situation her husband and son, not to mention all the other men of the manor, rode out to had rendered Iolanthe the soberest Rosamund had yet seen her.

■ ■ ■ ■

After much preparation, the men departed for battle. They looked formidable, but Rosamund wondered how many would not be returning at the fighting's end. In well-drilled formation, they marched out of the castle gates: mounted knights, foot soldiers with pikes and axes, longbowmen and archers, heading east to meet Baron de Mowbray's regrouped troops several miles hence, before turning north together toward the edge of Lord Parnell's land. They aimed ultimately for the errant magnate's own fortress, but if Parnell's own lookouts were of any quality at all, Lord Aelward's men would meet with opposition well before then.

For those left behind, the next days were subdued and grimly expectant. Those at the castle were all kept busy enough familiarizing themselves with their new stone surroundings, but it was not enough to diffuse the air of foreboding.

The worst aspect of battle, to those at home, was when the wounded, the dying, and the dead were returned. It was three days after the soldiers had set off when the first of these sorry men arrived. Squires brought the injured on horse-drawn litters. Those less seriously wounded, but still unable to fight, arrived on their own horses or on foot.

Three ground-level rooms in the castle had been cleared to create a makeshift infirmary. The castle servants still had their usual tasks to do, while the majority of village women were obliged to continue the farm labor that their menfolk had abandoned. Thus, it fell to those with the most time on their hands to assist Lord Aelward's personal physic by taking on the work of nursing, and so the ladies-in-waiting put aside their needlework and lessons and fell to the unhappy task. A few women from the village known to have skill with herbs and medicaments were also brought up to the castle to help.

It was not the first time that many of the women of the manor had seen the results of warfare, but it was the first time for Rosamund. At first, she was horrified by some of the injuries she saw. With trembling hands and waves of nausea threatening to overcome her, she washed wounds, removed debris, and learned to apply remedies and dressings under the auspices of the kindly village women. At the end of her first day, she could not eat her supper, nor could she eat any breakfast the day after. She retreated to her bedroom and collapsed to her knees on the stone floor, shaking. She could face nothing to eat again the next day despite feeling faint with exhaustion. By the end of the day a stout, practical woman by the name of Winifred, who managed to deal with the most alarming injuries with brisk competence, took Rosamund to task.

"For pity's sake, my dear, you must eat, or you will have no strength for the tasks ahead of you. Just a little. Try this, here." And she tore off some bread, waved it in front of Rosamund, and refused to cease badgering her until Rosamund had taken a few bites.

"Now some soup," Winifred insisted, gesturing at the bowl in front of Rosamund. Rosamund sipped halfheartedly at a spoonful, for it was easier than resisting the bombardment of encouragement.

"I was just the same," Winifred said to Rosamund as she enthusiastically tucked in to her own supper. "Fair takes the love of food quite from you. It gets better. You'll have your appetite back in a day or two. You'll see."

Rosamund could not imagine it. But Winifred proved to be right. Somehow, she began to become accustomed to the unpleasantness of the infirmary and did not mentally recoil each time she had to dress a wound. Her fingers trembled less. Somehow she managed to banish the feeling of panic and helplessness to the back of her mind and concentrate on the task in hand. She held back her tears for when she had finished her shift, and somehow they learned to stay away until then.

When she had a moment to take a rest, she would climb to the battlements to let the breeze cool her face and the noise of the castle courtyard fade a little with the distance. It was at one such moment that she saw it: the wagon of wounded, carrying one among them with blue and gold and the wing of a white eagle clearly visible on his surcoat.

Rosamund ran down the steps of the battlements so fast she nearly tripped and fell. She was one of the first to see the returned soldiers as the wagon entered the courtyard. Her heart pounding in dread, she hovered over the wagon gate as it was unfastened. In a second she saw that the blue and gold surcoat belonged not to Alexander, but to the dark head of Robert. Her utter relief at not finding Alexander among the wounded was immediately mixed with horror at finding the injured man to be her cousin.

Robert looked in a bad way. He had a large gash in his leg and another in his stomach, perhaps a pike wound that his mail had been unable to protect against. She could not tell if he was asleep or unconscious, but he made no effort to stir himself and was carried from the wagon. Rosamund led the way, directing his bearers to an unoccupied bed in the infirmary. She sought the physic immediately, then sent one of the chambermaids-turned-nurses to find her aunt and tell her the bad news. Trembling, the girl scurried away, obviously unhappy to be delivering such tidings about the manor's heir. Rosamund set to immediately, removing cloth and mail with the help of another nurse as gently as possible.

Within minutes she heard Iolanthe come running into the infirmary, hands clasped in fear over her mouth; she then knelt at Robert's bedside, one hand holding his own, the other smoothing his hair. She was crying, the first time Rosamund had seen her do so.

"We must do everything we can," Iolanthe was whispering. "The physic, where is the physic?"

"Here, my lady."

Iolanthe turned to him.

"How badly is he hurt?"

"I have only had a brief look at his wounds, my lady, but they are deep."

"Will he survive?"

"I cannot say, but I will do everything I can for him. He is young and strong; he has that much in his favor."

"Young and strong," repeated Iolanthe, her voice weak and wobbling. She began to cry again. The physic placed his hand gently on her shoulder.

"I must clean his wounds as best I can now. We will send news every hour." But Iolanthe refused to go, and she sat on a wooden stool by Robert's bed, holding his hand, while the physic worked.

Later, as Rosamund lay exhausted in her bed, she could not help but revisit her response to seeing the blue and gold of Duloe colors on the wagon of wounded. She had truly been in fear of finding Alexander dead or dying. She felt guilty for offering up a silent prayer of thanks for his continued preservation while Robert lay so ill. The frantic days had taken away her lingering preoccupation with Alexander, but at night he returned to her thoughts unbidden. Reflecting on the last few days' events, she had a far greater sense now of why Alexander was so serious. Why he did not light up with charm and smiles the instant she might engage him in conversation. Death was not a stranger to anybody in Rosamund's world, but Alexander must have seen so much violent death. To swear an oath to protect was to swear an oath to kill. What effect must it have on the heart after so many years? No longer could she feel quite so angry about Alexander's dalliance with Marie. She understood more keenly why Lord Aelward would insist everyone made merry at a feast while he made battle plans. Alexander, as well as most, was surely entitled to his occasional entertainments when he faced a life interposed with periods such as this.

Mercifully, by the end of the next day the flow of wounded into the castle had slowed considerably. Messengers arrived in their wake, bringing back the most welcome news that the battle was over. Lord Parnell's troops had been considerably depleted and the lord himself captured on the third day. He was being held at de Mowbray's own manor, thence to be taken swiftly to London for the king to dispense justice as he saw fit. It was an end to the hostilities, at least for the time being. The wave of relief around the castle was palpable.

Rosamund had been too busy in the infirmary to see the troops return, but she had heard the continual clatter of horses' hooves in the stable courtyard through the next afternoon.

When she had made her charge as comfortable as possible, Rosamund took a moment to herself and walked out to see what she could of the returning troops.

Her path out through an arched doorway was blocked by a figure coming the other way. Facing into the dark, she could not make out who it was for a moment. Then she nearly sank to her knees with the beating of her heart. It was Alexander. Seeing her halt so suddenly, he put out a hand to steady her. She shook her head to show she was fine.

"I could not see who you were in the gloom. I stopped to see . . ." she faltered. "You return unharmed," she said with avidity as she gazed at him, so relieved was she at the sight of him standing uninjured in front of her. "We are all so very gratified at your victory. It is blessed news."

For a moment Alexander merely stood, his expression unfathomable. Then he spoke.

"Thank you, Lady Rosamund. I feel the

fortune of it strongly. But I come to see those who have been less lucky." He took a few steps further into the light of the passageway. Rosamund could see the dirt on his face and garb, the pallor of exhaustion under the brown of his skin. She could hear the tones of weariness in his voice. He must only just have arrived, yet his first call was upon the men who had served him.

"I will show you the way," said Rosamund in a more practical manner, turning back the way she had come. Alexander followed her.

"You have seen Robert return?" he asked, drawing alongside her. Rosamund nodded unhappily.

"He has been moved to his room in the manor house. The physic is tending to him."

"What does he conclude?"

"He doesn't know how Robert will do. He said we should consider Robert's youth and strength."

Alexander shook his head. "There is little these physics can do. Yet I place my hopes in him as much as the next man."

"Why did Robert return wounded so late?" asked Rosamund. "We have not seen such serious injury for a day now and thought the worst of the close quarters battle wounds returned to us already."

Alexander sighed in annoyance.

"He refused to be taken back immediately after battle. He wanted to stay with the troops and insisted he would be fine. He would not have anyone take a look at that wound to his stomach until he collapsed. Damn fool." Alexander swore with concern.

He checked upon each wounded man in turn. If the man was awake, he leaned over to greet him quietly and thanked him for his service in battle. Rosamund noted how the men's eyes brightened a little at Alexander's praise. She could see how he must inspire respect in them on the battlefield, gratified as they were by his attention. Alexander said little to Rosamund as they traversed the sickrooms, but he listened attentively to her murmured commentary on how each man was doing. There was an intimacy in their shared task. Rosamund too felt somehow comforted by his solid presence, yet after they finished she turned to him, chiding gently:

"You should rest now. I can see how tired you are."

He looked a little nonplussed, then gave a brief smile.

"It is of no consequence, but you will tell me I ought to do as the infirmary nurse bids, so I will leave you in peace. Thank you for seeing the men with me."

He gave a bow and departed the way he had come, his footsteps ringing out across the stone underfoot.

Of course, care of the wounded did not end upon the return of the troops. While conversing with some of the men convalescing in the airiness of the courtyard one sunny morning two days later, Alexander saw Rosamund carrying some food to a man still unable to walk. Her hair was held off her face in its long chestnut plait, her apron cinched in to reveal the slenderness of her waist. Up until this battle he would guess she had seen little of the savagery of death caused by conflict. The last few days would have changed all that, yet still she had an air of serenity about her. She smiled at the man as she laid the food in his lap and adjusted the cushion behind him to help him sit more comfortably. Then she straightened up, looking around to see whom else she might assist. The man looked at her gratefully, his gaze lingering upon her a little longer after she left him. A man would have to be half blind not to see her pulchritude, he thought, even dressed as plainly as she was.

■ ■ ■ ■

Robert was not recovering quickly from his wound. He lay on his bed, his face as pale as the sheet beneath him.

"The physic fears an infection has set in," whispered Maud from behind Rosamund's shoulder.

"Is it serious?"

"Aye. Mayhap he'll pull through, but once it gets into the blood there's nothing that can be done. A few recover still. Most do not."

Maud's face was grim. Then she said, "Winifred believes there might be a poultice of agrimony that can help, but she hasn't enough of the herb to make it."

"Then we must get some."

"She says there is none to be found except several miles north or so, back toward Parnell's land."

"Can a party not still go? We should propose it."

Conflicting emotions crossed Iolanthe's face as she talked to Rosamund in her bower.

"We must get some of these herbs Winifred has spoken of," said Rosamund, urgency in her voice. "Robert must have something for the fever. Winifred has taught me much about her herbs and flowers in the last few days. In any case, I would know the right one if I saw it. I will go."

"As if your lordship would have you running around in the meadows at a time like this!" exclaimed her aunt.

"Please, Lady Aelward, I beg you. No one else can find the flowers as quickly as I can. Winifred is unwell; she is elderly and exhausted by her efforts these last few days. Everyone else has many burdens at this minute, but I do not. I pray you let me go. It will not take more than a day at the most."

Iolanthe sighed. "You make a goodly argument, my dear. I hate to spare you, and I have no idea yet what your uncle will say when he hears of this, for it is hardly the task of a lady-in-waiting, but I confess I would have this done for Robert. Very well, prepare in haste."

Rosamund hugged her aunt tightly. "Thank you. I will return safely, I promise."

Iolanthe looked unconvinced despite Rosamund's reassurance.

"If it must be done, I will ask Alexander to head your party. I trust him above all others to keep you safe. And he will want to do all he can for Robert; that I know."

Their party set out shortly afterward, with

the soldiers well provisioned for the ride. Despite it being mid-afternoon, the June sun had abandoned them, and the gray clouds above threatened rain as they trotted out of the gates.

CHAPTER TEN

Rosamund insisted on riding by herself and taking a bow and quiver, for she had learned some archery under her brothers' tutelage at home. Under the circumstances, her decision went unquestioned and her weaponry was scarcely noticed.

Her escort was also well armed. To begin with, they headed northeast on relatively well-traveled paths. A few hours later they passed a small village and then turned off onto smaller tracks toward the hamlet of Pilning as Winifred had instructed. This took another hour. They did not stop in the village, though its inhabitants came out, curious about the strangers passing their way.

"As long as none is loyal to Parnell," muttered Alexander grimly.

Winifred had predicted the beginning of higher ground not far after the hamlet, and sure enough their path began to rise a little.

Going ever deeper into the thickening woodland, their path soon faded to a thin track, reflecting the infrequency of journeys into the wood from the hamlet. Rosamund was just starting to feel a sense of uncertainty about their direction when the party almost literally rode into a wall of rock rising above them about twenty feet. Winifred had talked of this: a backbone of rock running north to south that started just north of Pilning, and they had clearly reached it. It was passable in places, but her intention was to have them ascend higher onto the rock. Here, protected a little by higher outcrops but allowed sunshine by the lack of trees, Winifred had heard that the agrimony they sought could be found.

They stopped, and Alexander signaled for them to dismount and start the search. Rosamund started climbing sure-footedly over the boulders that littered the ground and onto the main body of rock. Alexander followed.

They both saw the open ground at the same time, and Rosamund gave a small exclamation of relief when she saw the plants she was seeking, nestling among the grass. She smiled in confirmation of Alexander's questioning look, then knelt down and carefully started pinching off the leaves she needed and depositing them in a little knapsack she had brought with her. Twenty minutes of searching and picking was enough to gather sufficient quantities of the herb to treat Robert and any other injured man besides. She was just straightening up when the unpleasantly familiar zing of an arrow whipped past her head. Alexander heard it too.

"Get down!" he shouted, but she had already thrown herself to the ground instinctively. There was far too little cover for them to be safe. As another arrow flew past them, Alexander was decisive.

"Run! That way." He pointed west, back down the rocky scree into the thick of the wood. "And keep low." Rosamund hitched up her skirts and peeled away. She could hear Alexander scrambling down behind her, but as they reached the lower tree cover again, they found themselves right upon two soldiers on horseback. Although dismounted, Alexander still had his sword and his armor; Rosamund had her bow and quiver. Their only other advantage was the closeness of the trees amidst which their attackers maneuvered. The closest of the horsemen made to strike at Alexander, but his blow was softened by the limited space in which to swing his sword. Alexander's own sword was already drawn and ready to parry as he yelled to Rosamund.

"Keep running!" With no experience of defending herself from mounted attack she did so, fleeing as fast as she could, heading into the trees and crashing through the low, thin branches, which whipped at her. Despite her pace, she felt the grip of fear as she heard the sound of hoofbeats behind her. The second horseman must be following her. Despite the trees, he was making headway toward her. She zigzagged to where she thought the trees were thickest, for she knew if she kept some trees between them, a man on horseback would have difficulty catching her. Then, to her dismay, a fallen tree trunk tripped her and she fell. Her pursuer was very close behind now; she could hear the horse's breath. As she turned to see if she could recover in time to put a distance between them again, she saw she could not. There was only one option left to her: she loosed an arrow with a swiftness born of fear as well as practice. Whether by luck or judgment, she caught her pursuer on the shoulder. He fell from his horse with a cry, his steed whinnying and cartwheeling without its rider. Rosamund gathered up her skirts and bow and ran on, pushing through twigs and branches and stumbling over more roots until she felt she had put a good distance between herself and her unseated enemy. Halting, she crouched down next to a tree trunk, her breath coming in ragged gasps. She tried to steady her breathing so she could listen. All was quiet except for the chirping of birds. She was probably a good distance from her own party now, but she was most uncertain of the safety of returning in that direction. She continued to sit with the unnatural stillness of the hunted for some minutes, her heart hammering in her chest, on the utmost alert for any further trouble. She was just wondering what she ought to do next when she heard someone calling her name faintly in the distance. She almost sagged with relief, then struggled up and set off with trepidation in the direction from which she thought she had heard the call. After a minute she stopped again, uncertain of her heading. Thankfully, she heard the call again, this time closer, and set off again quickly.

"Over here!" she called back, going as quickly as she could on the uneven ground, for she knew it was dangerous to be drawing attention to themselves in such a way, and she owed it to her companions to respond before a foe could take advantage. Within another minute she had broken out into a clearing, formed where the stony ground started again. She must be close to the rocky backbone once more. Across the way, she was infinitely glad to catch sight of Alexander and his squire, William. But before either could run across to her, there was a rush of air and a crack as an arrow sped across the clearing and hit a tree close to Rosamund's head. Instinctively, she threw herself to the ground again. Lying on her stomach, her hands grasping soil, she heard men's roars and the sound of running. She heard the clash of swords, and then a desperate cry that she knew could be nothing other than a fatally wounded man. There was the sound of more crashing through trees and then what she thought was Alexander calling commands. The next moment a body landed right by her; she screamed, but the next instant she heard Alexander's voice in her ear saying urgently:

"It is I; keep down." He swept his cloak over her, lying so close he was almost on top of her, an arm over her back as though to caution her to stay down. It seemed like an eternity that she lay there, her blood rushing, staring at a tiny green sapling struggling to grow on the forest floor. Its greenness and newness seemed the utmost contrast to the activity happening only yards away. The noise died away, and suddenly Alexander rose to kneel next to her, still as stone for what seemed like an age, though it was probably only a minute before he moved again. He swept his cloak back over his shoulder and stood up.

"You can get up now," he said gently. With a sense of unreality Rosamund reluctantly relinquished her patch of forest floor, brushing dirt, moss, and woody fragments from her palms and taking his proffered hand. With an arm around her shoulders he led her to a natural ledge of the rocky outcrop and bade her sit down. She was only too glad to.

Shortly after, William rounded the corner followed by the other men and the horses, and gave a brief report.

"Lord's Parnell's men by the livery, three of them. Two dead." At this he glanced quickly at Rosamund but continued. "One is injured, but he made off through the trees. I have sent the rest of the men after him; he won't get far." He added to Rosamund, "We mean to capture him if we can, not kill him. We can use him in barter for peace." Rosamund nodded automatically, as though she were well familiar with battle parleys and hostage exchange. It hardly seemed the time to ask questions, and she wanted to think as little as possible about the short but bloody exchange that had just taken place. But she wondered if they would care to know about her own encounter.

"I was chased by one of the two riders who attacked Lord Ringewar and me to begin with," she volunteered. "I shot him. In the shoulder, and he fell. I couldn't tell you exactly where, for I ran awhile until I heard you calling."

"Brave girl," said Alexander. "It was a party of four, then. Have you any idea in which direction he might be?"

"I ran as straight as I could," said Rosamund, "which may not be very straight at all, but it was the opposite way from which you came into the clearing. I fear I cannot be more help than that."

"I will pursue it," said William. "Shall we reconnoiter here?" he added to Alexander, who nodded his agreement. He then looked through the trees up at the sky. The shadows were getting longer, and Rosamund realized it was less than an hour before sundown.

"It is too late to travel back to the castle before night," Alexander said, "and I would prefer not to rest in the closest village."

"Nor I," agreed William. "They must have done exactly what you hoped they would not and informed our enemy of our presence.

"Like as not they were in the village already, the villagers too scared to say anything." Alexander scowled. "Parnell has spread his influence wide."

"Lord Alexander, shall I now leave you with the lady and pursue our final quarry?" asked William. "He is unlikely to pose much of a threat if he is shot."

"With my willing permission," Alexander replied. "Take care, and prepare a bird's call on your return so I will know friend from foe."

With a nod, William and the other soldiers melted into the trees and were soon swallowed up by the rapidly advancing gloom.

Bidding Rosamund to stay by the rock, Alexander conducted a thorough reconnoiter of his own around the area. Returning, he deemed it safe enough to begin unpacking a few belongings from the horses' panniers. Rosamund made to help, but he placed a hand upon her arm to deter her.

"You will surely have had enough exertion for one afternoon," he said. "Pray rest."

"I would prefer to act than rest," said Rosamund truthfully, for the shock of the afternoon remained, and she was reluctant to give her thoughts time to rest squarely upon the frightening events for fear of her reaction.

Alexander took one look at her pale face.

"I am deeply sorry, Lady Rosamund. This afternoon is a brutish interlude of the kind I hoped we would avoid."

His voice was soft, and to Rosamund's dismay it released bitter words from her that a sterner tone might have stemmed.

"I will admit it," she said. "It has disturbed me deeply. To be shot at and chased for no reason other than because I seek to help my own kin. These feuds and power struggles cause nothing but harm." Stony faced, she sat back down upon the ledge. "I will never understand how men come to kill so easily."

"I cannot speak for these other men," said Alexander, "but I do not find it easy. I have no desire to kill my fellow countryman, but if he is to turn on me and those I love, then I am sworn to protect them and myself. I abhor it, but it is my duty."

"Then wherein lies the strangeness of these men who start the fighting? Are they so unusual, such abominations of nature, to make war?" said Rosamund angrily. "There is nothing unusual in this; there is always fighting among men. If not one year, then a decade hence will undoubtedly prove it so."

"You make us sound like animals with nothing in our hearts but war," chided Alexander. "Do not do men such a disservice as to think we have no care for anything but death; you must know that to be untrue."

"I know no such thing," Rosamund snapped. "Men are fighting men once more, and we are all suffering because of it." She turned her head wildly. "Where will you bury those poor mothers' sons tonight?"

"Those poor mothers' sons wished to kill me and would have killed you if they had had a better chance," was Alexander's curt reply.

But Rosamund did not listen; she was suddenly horrified by the thought that the man she had shot with an arrow might now be dead by her own hand. She fervently hoped not. She knew that Alexander's protest that he was caught up in the situation of defending himself was exactly the same reason why she had loosed her arrow, and it pained her yet further to think of herself as a part of such violence. The initial numbness in her mind had quite worn off, and the horrors of the day rose up in her mind. Tears pricked at her eyelids. She turned away from Alexander and walked swiftly away to hide her weakness. Sheltering by a rocky outcrop, she had stifled no more than a couple of sobs when she heard him come after her. She refused to look at him as he approached and stopped close.

She wiped her cheeks with her handkerchief. "Forgive me," she said sternly, "I have said much in haste."

"There is nothing to forgive, except my own words," he said kindly.

Rosamund shook her head. "Doubtless you think I am a foolish, pampered creature with naïve presumptions of the world. And perhaps I am." She wiped her face again and tossed her head as if to shake off her unhappy mood.

"Nonsense," Alexander exclaimed. "You are entirely unused to things such as we have seen today. It would be a shock for anyone. I myself have been ill at the sight of battle, and not simply the first time. It is not foolish to be overwhelmed by the enormity of death."

At his last words her tears threatened to overcome her attempt at bravado and her face crumpled again.

"There!" Alexander was clearly annoyed at himself. "I have gone and upset you again. I am of no comfort. Ah!" Running short of words with which to make her feel better, he instinctively leaned toward her to stroke her hair with his hand. Such an unexpected expression of concern only made Rosamund's tears flow faster, at which point he gently took her in his arms and held her. Grateful for the warm, strong sense of comfort his physical presence brought after such distress, she was powerless to resist. She willingly abandoned herself to his embrace and clung to him, heedless of the utter lack of decorum with which she acted.

Alexander's jaw rubbed softly against Rosamund's temple; he held her closer and somehow she could not help but turn her face up to him, the source of her comfort, like a flower would to the sun. Whether he had meant only to comfort her, it was too late: as if of their own accord, his hands reached up to trace the contours of her face wonderingly. Then he whispered her name tenderly, longingly, before pressing his mouth to hers.

The noise of people approaching broke in on them. Faint from the moment, Rosamund had to drag herself back to their wider reality. Alexander was releasing her and already giving a bird call signal in reply. At the sound of someone approaching around the rock, they both instinctively stepped a little distance away from each other. William appeared.

"We found your man," he said to Rosamund. "Injured but alive. We have dressed his wounds and brought him back here. He will travel back with us tomorrow." He seemed to sense nothing of the atmosphere between Rosamund and Alexander.

"We will camp down for the night here," said Alexander to William, and with but a brief glance to Rosamund who could not, in her shattered composure, even attempt to meet his eye, he turned away to continue with his preparations.

Rosamund spent a restless night lying under rough blankets with a padded saddle pack for a pillow. As her head spun with the events of the day, she had wondered if she would fall asleep at all, but a fitful slumber finally descended upon her. She awoke early, just before dawn, at the sound of the men moving about. She shifted. Her joints felt stiff. She was used to the aches of physical exercise, but a bed of hard ground cushioned but a little by blankets was hardly conducive to a comfortable night's sleep. As she sat up, Alexander, already up and seeing her awake, came over. At the sight of him, she recalled the events of the previous day in a rush and could only hope the cloak she had pulled around her disguised the dull flush that surely colored her face.

"The men are preparing a small breakfast," he said in a cordial manner. "In the meantime, there is a small stream about thirty yards that way if you care to refresh yourself." He pointed away into the forest. "I will escort you, though we believe it to be safe enough for now."

"Thank you," said Rosamund, noting that he seemed able to talk to her in a perfectly ordinary fashion. He offered her a hand to get up. Despite the hour and the tiredness that she had not yet shaken off, she found her awareness sharpen as she took it. She folded the blankets she had slept with and left them in a little pile on a large stone so as not to dampen them further on the dewy ground. Alexander led the way to the small stream and then retreated, saying he would wait ten yards hence until she returned.

In the cold of the morning and the knowledge that Alexander hovered but a few yards away, Rosamund decided upon a plan of merely cleaning her hands and face, and rubbing a finger around her teeth. She brushed out her hair as best she could with her fingers and then tied it back again, returning to Alexander after she had done so. With a polite nod, he started on the way back to the encampment in silence.

Rosamund was full of confusion and a dawning disappointment. She did not know what she had expected him to say, nor what she had expected to happen next between them, but she realized she had anticipated an acknowledgement of some kind of yesterday's intimacy. Perhaps he was merely being discreet, as he had been about their first woodland meeting. It would be the simplest response to their indiscretion. Yet did she really want him to act as though nothing had happened, as though it were not of the merest consequence to him? Her answer was an immediate no.

Still he did not speak. A creeping dread stole over her. Surely if he returned her feelings even in the smallest measure, he would have spoken of it? If he gave no impression of any tender emotion within him at the break of the new day, it boded poorly of any affection on his part. How else could she interpret his silence? Was he not at this moment forsaking a perfect chance to declare himself?

On her return, she was handed a cup and plate by William and, with a muted thanks, she busied herself with a meager breakfast of dry bread and salted meat, washed down with water from the stream. The men continued to pack up their few belongings, and shortly afterwards the party set off on their way home.

It was an uneventful journey that gave time for reflection, but Rosamund was no closer to resolving her conflicting emotions as they finally approached Duloe. Miserably, her head churning with ever more misgivings as they traveled, she had begun to fear that Alexander's silence when they were alone that morning indicated a lack of esteem for her, for a woman who would so readily kiss a man the moment such an opportunity arose. Rosamund shuddered to think of what unsavory disposition he might now attribute to her. He could hardly be blamed for having the impression that no apology from him was either expected or deserved. It was an unhappy thought.

No sooner were they admitted through the castle gates than Rosamund was shepherded off by her aunt amidst a great clucking of concern, away from the magnetic, disturbing presence of Alexander Ringewar.

CHAPTER ELEVEN

Lord Robert was gravely ill now; the infection had taken a strong hold in Rosamund's absence. His breath was shallow and fast, and his skin burned with fever. From the look in the physic's eyes, Rosamund saw with a little start of fear that he had no cure and precious little confidence in his patient's recovery. She hoped that Winifred was making speedily with the agrimony. It might be Robert's only chance.

For two more days and nights, Robert's life hung in the balance. Iolanthe and Lord Aelward kept a constant vigil by his bedside. The chaplain visited often to bless him. Milicent had lost all of her usual querulousness and was only to be found pale-cheeked and hollow-eyed at his bedside or tear-streaked in the chapel. Rosamund did her best to help by spending time with the children, who wanted to know when their father would be better and when their mother might be persuaded to play with them again.

On her return, Rosamund sat at a little wooden desk in the solar, writing a letter to fill the time while no patient required her attentions. Lord Aelward would undoubtedly have sent word to her family of the impending hostilities, and hopefully of their recent conclusion, but she knew that her mother, in particular, would be desperate to hear news of Rosamund's good health from Rosamund herself. The composition of the letter, however, necessitated a decision on how much detail to include of her own adventurings, and Rosamund's thoughts returned once again to the stolen kiss in the forest and her feelings for the inscrutable Alexander.

She had not seen him since their return from Pilning. On one hand, she was relieved; on the other, she found herself resentful that he had taken no opportunity to resolve the social impropriety that, to her mind, hung over her like an invisible cloud. Rosamund was unconsciously hardening her heart over Alexander. Anger was building within her, anger toward him but also toward herself for falling for someone who could apparently act in such a way toward her. She was no different than Marie now, except that she, Rosamund, ought to know better, whereas Marie was merely a servant girl and no one would hold her up to such high standards. Maud's words from their first meal together at Duloe came back to her: so many women seemed to fall for Alexander, but he had not reciprocated their feelings. Why had she ever thought he would reciprocate hers? Yet she could still not shake off the memory of how it had felt to be held in his arms.

Unconsciously, she raised a palm to her cheek, flushing in guilty recollection. Her fear remained that he would not now think she deserved the respect a lady was ordinarily due. She had certainly given him cause to doubt it. Perhaps even now he was talking about her with the other men, recounting the amusing diversion. No, she could only pray that Alexander were a gentleman about it. Shaking herself, she tried to put it out of her mind by turning once more to her letter. She had completed only a few more sentences before she was disturbed by the sound of footsteps on the flagstones. These heralded the arrival of Maud, pink-cheeked and wide-eyed.

"It is Lord Robert! He wakes! The physic thinks he has turned for the better. Do

183

come!" Rosamund dropped her pen and obeyed Maud's beckoning.

Rosamund and Maud clattered up the nearest staircase to the room where Robert lay. His family was already with him, and while Rosamund and Maud did not dare enter to disturb them, they saw Iolanthe's strained but smiling face turn toward them in the doorway to confirm the good news.

"The fever has broken," confirmed the physic.

Flooded with relief, Rosamund took a moment to smile in return at her aunt's good cheer before turning away to leave them in peace.

As she turned, she nearly walked into a person behind her, also come at the news of Robert's awakening. It was Alexander.

They both stepped back from one another, the boundaries of propriety rigidly preserved this time.

"How is he? I have heard he has awoken," said Alexander.

"Yes, it would seem," said Rosamund. "It is all good news."

"I made my way as quickly as I could," continued Alexander. He moved to the doorframe and made to enter and pay his respects.

He had lost none of his arresting presence.

With her heart beating a little at the unexpected encounter, Rosamund thanked Maud and then melted away toward the staircase, intending to return to the solar. She was walking down the passageway and back to her letter when she heard footsteps behind her.

"Lady Rosamund!" It was Alexander. Out of courtesy she could do nothing but turn to face him.

"I would not stay and be a nuisance to Lord Robert," he said, approaching her, "and this seemed as good an occasion as any on which to talk to you in peace. Are you busy?"

Rosamund shook her head. "I write a letter to my family," she replied truthfully.

"Then I will not keep you long," said Alexander, "but before you go I must apologize. For what has happened between us. You know of what I speak, I am sure."

Rosamund hesitated, uncertain of how to respond. His presence and the attention he was directing so firmly toward her disconcerted her, as usual, and she had no precedent for discussing so intimate a subject with a man who perturbed her so.

"First, I acknowledge my discourtesy for saying nothing on the morn of our stay in the woods," Alexander continued in the absence of any response from her. "I should have spoken of what transpired, but I was more concerned with our safety than with tarrying to converse. Perhaps it was a misjudgment, as I ought to have sought your forgiveness more promptly. And, more important, I hope that you will forgive me for the impropriety of the previous day and that we might put it behind us."

At his words, Rosamund suddenly felt deflated. She had indeed been crushed by his silence, and it had preyed on her mind. Yet now as he spoke, she finally knew by his words and his tone that he must regret his actions. Here was confirmation that he wished he had not kissed her. In which case he had no feelings for her. She felt like a complete fool. Anger rose up in a protective rush against the hurtful realization.

"You may rest assured it will not happen again," Alexander continued in grave tones.

In her hurt, Rosamund gave a tiny laugh of derision.

"I should think not. Not with me, at least."

Alexander paused and looked at her searchingly. "You say that as though I make a habit of behaving in such a way."

"Do you not?" snapped Rosamund.

"I assure you I do not." Alexander replied a little coldly. "I understand your anger because of the way I have treated you, but I must protest if you are left with an impression that I act in such a way in a regular fashion. I hold the virtues of chivalry and esteem for all women very highly."

"Esteem for all women, indeed," Rosamund flared suddenly. "I only suppose it doesn't extend as far as cavorting with serving girls and noblewomen as you please. Or is that an aspect of chivalry that I fail to understand?"

"Serving girls?" Alexander frowned in confusion.

"Very well; one serving girl," amended Rosamund shrewishly. "I am referring to one of the servings girls at Duloe. Marie," she continued, still seeing only blankness in his expression. Then in her impatience she blurted out, "Did you not . . ." She could not bring herself to say what she needed to say to extract a confession from him that would condemn his hypocrisy.

"Did I not what?" Alexander frowned with curiosity at her unfinished sentence.

"Did you not . . . flirt abominably with the serving girl Marie, at the castle, on the night of the May feast? And more besides, if a tale I have heard is to be believed? Is that the chaste behavior referred to by your redoubtable chivalric code?"

Alexander gave a short, unamused laugh.

"In answer to both parts of your question, no and no again. What in heaven's name gave you that idea? No, wait." He held up his hand and continued in a voice tinged with scorn. "I can imagine. I do remember talking to a serving wench by the fire after the feast. Is that the Marie to whom you refer?" Rosamund nodded a mute assent.

"Well, we danced a reel or two after that," continued Alexander. "She was pretty and of a lively sort. We talked and jested and danced. But nothing else happened." His eyes were hard as he gazed upon her. "And if I am to reveal all to you, then I had the impression that she was a little taken with another man. If I remember rightly, shortly after I excused myself to find further victuals, I returned and saw she was sitting on the knee of another of your uncle's men-at-arms, and then I saw no more of them. It was of no personal concern to me. Shortly after that your uncle summoned me to discuss our strategy for the coming days. You may ask him yourself if you doubt my word. Or ask the girl herself. Or Sir Gawain DeFevre, should you require the testimony of the other pertinent witness.

"But yes, I can imagine that inquisitive eyes that night, seeing me conversing in lighthearted tones with a pretty serving wench, could conjure up a tale for busy mouths to pass on." Alexander sounded yet more scathing at this. "It becomes ever clearer to me that sometimes there is little for the inhabitants of this manor to talk about save for what they invent for themselves. If we were all judged on the hearsay of others, we would doubtless measure up most poorly indeed."

Unnerved as she was by his anger, Rosamund could not help but feel relief at his rejection of the charge she had lain at his door. To think of the time she had wasted in her unhappy jealousy of Marie. A pity it changed nothing of his feelings for her — except that now he would think yet worse of her for accusing him of such behavior. Why could she not control her anger when it came to Alexander? Her jealousy had undermined all her own virtues of reasonableness and agreeableness. She squared her shoulders at his deserved attack, her own anger extinguished by his words.

"Well then, I am sorry to have charged you unjustly."

Alexander calmed himself a little, noticing the downturn of her mouth.

"Well, I cannot blame you," he laughed bitterly. "For there was little to commend me to you by any account in Pilning."

"On the contrary," said Rosamund begrudgingly. "You acted to protect me that day when we encountered Lord Parnell's soldiers, and I owe you a debt. For that I ought thank you, not berate you."

"I did my duty, nothing more," replied Alexander in a more conciliatory manner. "But as for the other, my apology stands. I behaved unchivalrously. Now shall we declare a ceasefire on the matter and have done with it?" His voice was kindlier now. Rosamund was still downcast by his desire to dismiss the incident, but she could gain nothing further from their exchange except to capitulate with what little dignity she had left. She counseled herself that her best option was to be as gracious as he, to pretend their kiss was indeed an unfortunate aberration elicited by nothing other than the heightened emotions of armed conflict. She nodded her assent.

"It is forgotten."

But she knew, for her own part at least, that forgetting would be an impossibility.

Prior to the news of Robert's recovery, Alexander had spent the morning in a poor mood. He had snapped uncustomarily at his squire for overfeeding their horses. He knew he was tired both from the exertions of the past days and many broken nights' sleep, but there was also another issue on his mind.

Since their journey home to Duloe, Alexander had found himself distracted by thoughts of Rosamund more often than was comfortable. He was angry with himself for not controlling better the urge to kiss her. But as for the moment itself, holding her in his arms had been nothing but pleasurable, though he knew he owed her an apology for the sake of courtesy. Priding himself on his manners, he was also deeply unsatisfied with his decision not to mention their tryst the first chance he had had the next morning. Worried as he had been about their safety, with hindsight he would have done better by her to apologize for his amorous imposition immediately. For by his cursory knowledge of her character since first meeting her, he blamed himself entirely for the kiss in the forest. He should not have taken advantage of her during such a vulnerable moment. She had clearly not been herself.

After their conversation by the infirmary, he felt a little happier about the whole business. He was glad to have found an opportunity to speak to her, for the days had been uncommonly busy since their return to Duloe. The men-at-arms were entirely taken up in the aftermath of battle. Horses needed tending, armor and weapons fixing and refitting, and milder strains and sprains needed to be rested. For the most part, the female family members had also been taking their meals in private while Lord Robert's health remained precarious. Encountering Rosamund outside Robert's bedchamber had provided the first private opportunity to talk to her about such a personal matter.

Her anger at his own behavior toward her was quite understandable. He felt some satisfaction at the thought that Rosamund was not as free with her affections as some noblewomen he had encountered, who treated courtly love as an excuse for adultery and licentiousness and whose moral respectability was but a surface gild.

As for rumors about his conduct with a serving girl, well, he was used to castle gossip. Yet he had certainly been surprised by Rosamund's accusation over Marie. Much as he was angry to find that his honor had been questioned more deeply than it ought, his curiosity was piqued when he wondered why Rosamund had chosen to mention it. In addition, the fact that Rosamund herself had thought badly of him had filled him with a sense of injustice, for he had to admit he cared for her good opinion. He suspected he knew the reason why if he looked square upon the evidence. It concerned those flashing almond eyes of hers and her soft chestnut hair. It would involve that willowy figure that she carried with energy and yet such grace. It would involve that generous mouth with its cupid's bow and quick smile. But that was not all. If he thought yet further, he could remember all else he admired about her: how she had galloped across the fields without a fear to be seen and thrown her head back in joyous laughter on the day he had seen her riding with Robert. What a contrast she had seemed to the painted mademoiselles of the royal court, with their coquettishness, their murmuring voices, and their simpering smiles. And he could not forget how she had tended to wounded soldiers with such tenderness. How she had dressed wounds even he would not have cared to look at for too long, without a thought for the blood on her clothes. How even now, he realized suddenly, he still wanted to take her in his arms and comfort her, obliterating the sights and sounds that had brought tears to her eyes in the forest in Pilning. Yes, if he thought overmuch about it, he could comprehend all the reasons why Rosamund's good opinion had any significance to him. But these were not times in which he could indulge himself in romantic idlings. If his heart were true to his code of honor, he must commit himself wholeheartedly to his duty, to give his liege his full dedication until the threat of these dangerous times had passed for certain.

It was only a little while later, as she sat unseeing at the solar desk once more, that Rosamund realized the full import of Alexander's refutation of any dalliance with Marie. If he spoke the truth — and she had no hesitation in believing him — it meant that he had not been echoing empty tributes to the virtues of chivalry nor broken any vows to which he claimed to be bound. When she had believed his virtuous protestations hollow, she had been able to use her disdain to defend herself against her attraction to him. Now that weapon was lost to her, at the very same time that she had to accept he had no wish to pursue her attentions past one regretted kiss.

Looking back to her unfinished letter, she remembered her mother's entreaty to behave well at Duloe. With the exception of these awkward episodes with Alexander, she had done so to the best of her ability. There and then she determined that she would put this latest indiscretion behind her. If she knew anything of Alexander, she could be confident that he would say nothing of it. If he thought the less of her for it, then she must bear it with good grace and remember to comport herself better in the future. The best she could now do was to behave toward him with gentility and charm, as she was obliged to act with all at Duloe. She set herself back to her letter writing with diligence.

For several days, Rosamund chanced not to see Alexander again in any capacity in which she might pursue her resolve of polite friendliness. She knew Alexander had visited his wounded men in the infirmary on several occasions, but it had always been in her absence. Whether this was by luck or judgment she could not say.

With Lord Robert's turn for the better, however, Lord Aelward commanded his family and retinue to return to their customary habit of eating in the Great Hall, albeit the new hall at the castle, and retiring together to converse in the evenings. Rosamund felt this her chance to start afresh with Alexander, to convince him that she did possess a little more poise than she had exhibited in recent weeks.

But her intentions came to naught.

His seat was empty at the next dinner they all took together, and there was no sign of him on the castle lawns in the evening.

"Does Lord Ringewar not join us?" asked Lady Gregory, as they strolled.

Lady Iolanthe turned to her. "You will not have heard yet, Alice."

"Heard what?" was Lady Gregory's reply. Overhearing the exchange, Rosamund hovered close enough to hear Iolanthe's response.

"Lord Ringewar received most troubling news this morning. His brother has been badly wounded in France. He had his squire saddle up his horse for an urgent journey and is gone."

CHAPTER TWELVE

"Gone?" echoed Rosamund, unable to help herself.

"Gone to Wickford," interjected Lord Aelward as he joined them. "A messenger arrived this morning from Wickford with news that his brother is badly hurt. An accident in France. Lord Ringewar has returned to his family seat to await further news."

"Lord bless him, he asked if we would prefer he wait until Robert were better mended before leaving, but we assured him it was not necessary," said Lady Iolanthe. "It is ill timed too. Just as we shed some care for Robert, now Lord Ringewar must take on the burden of another such worry."

"We must all pray for him and his brother," said Alice soberly.

Indeed I will, thought Rosamund fervently, trying to push her unworthy disappointment aside as they all murmured their sympathies for him.

■ ■ ■ ■

After Alexander's departure, it was as though the weather itself conspired to make Rosamund's heart heavier than ever. It rained almost ceaselessly for three weeks. The days were grey and wet; riding was an impossibility, and the gloom and tedium of being stuck inside the dingy castle walls all day, all underfoot of each other, infected the castle's inhabitants with melancholy and irritation in equal measure.

"Curse this infernal rain," growled Lord Aelward. "I do believe it is God's own joke to see how long we can be cooped up in here without taking our swords to one another."

"I don't have a sword, dear," replied Lady Aelward, a little peevishly. "And I am not sure if rain can actually be infernal when by its very nature it is rather cold and wet."

"For heaven's sake, woman." Lord Aelward raised his voice in annoyance. "You provide the perfect example of how we shall all be driven quite mad by one another. It was a figure of speech."

"There's no need to raise your voice," Lady Aelward rejoindered. "It was you that made the error, not I."

Lord Aelward's reply was to poke the afternoon fire with such force that embers flew out onto his hose. He hopped about, brushing them off and cursing loudly.

"But I am quite in agreement with you, my dear," added his wife, observing this display. "We need some distraction badly, for I cannot bear another afternoon of you stamping about complaining about the weather."

Fortunately, a distraction was nearly upon them.

Duloe was about to be graced with the esteemed presence of the Duke and Duchess of Marwickshire. Rosamund learned that the duke and his retinue were to reside at Duloe for a month before making their way onward to London to spend another month at the royal court. Duloe was a convenient stopping point and would be so again on their way home later in the summer. In total, there would be twenty extra mouths to feed, including some of the duke's relatives, the duchess' ladies-in-waiting, the duke's footmen, a wardrobe mistress, personal maids and servants, and the horsemen and guards. Lady Iolanthe had been entirely taken up with the preparations for the past fortnight. She whisked around the castle, chivvying servants and flapping her arms at her ladies-in-waiting, throwing out doom-laden prophesies as she went.

"We will never be ready, heaven save us, and the duchess will be sleeping on straw like a commoner," she would cry, before disappearing out of the room in a flurry of anxiety.

"See here!" she would scold a passing servant. "Candles nearly burned down to the quick. The duke will be tumbling down the stairs in the darkness, and our heads will roll after him, let there be no doubt about it!"

Maud confided to Rosamund her belief that, for all her panic and worry, Iolanthe secretly enjoyed the drama and the excitement, as well as the social merry-go-round of the actual visit. In truth, they were all looking forward to some novel company.

Thankfully, the noble party rolled in on a day when the rain clouds had withdrawn, leaving the summer sun to bathe the Duloe landscape in its honeyed rays. Rosamund and the other women were ready in their best day gowns to receive their visitors.

Alighting from their wagon, the duke and duchess were gracious of manner, reserved but not haughty. Likable enough, thought

Rosamund, admiring the duchess' intelligent gaze.

She was less impressed when introduced to Lady Henry, a cousin of the duke's and a companion for the duchess. Lady Henry barely smiled at Rosamund, flicking coldly discerning blue eyes over her briefly before moving on. Rosamund could not help but feel snubbed even though she knew her rank credited her with but a little social standing.

Next she was introduced to Lady Henry's daughter. Rosamund was struck by the beauty of the young woman. She had dark, almost black hair that contrasted flatteringly with her smooth, pale skin. Her eyes were the bright blue of her mother's, emphasized by curving dark lashes and brows. Her cheeks were blushed with the rose-petal pink hue of good health. On first greeting, she was far friendlier than her mother and greeted Rosamund with a charming smile.

"You are Lord Aelward's niece by his sister, are you not? I was told you were pretty; I was not misinformed."

Rosamund was disarmed by the unexpected compliment.

"Thank you, you flatter me," she managed with a small laugh. Perhaps she should have returned the compliment, but the moment passed and Sabeline's attention had been directed toward another new face.

When the introductions were finally complete, Iolanthe charged her ladies-in-waiting with escorting her guests to their rooms and with seeing to anything they might need. It fell to Rosamund to take care of the Henrys.

With the greatest of charm, Sabeline managed to keep Rosamund busy for the entire hour and a half before lunch with a string of requests: fetching her a drink, showing their personal maid the wardrobe facilities, delivering messages to various other members of the visiting party, changing a pillow that was "a touch too hard for my liking, and I should not wish to wake with a headache. Would you, Lady Rosamund?" Sabeline also insisted Rosamund stay to give her opinion on several different hairstyles that she pronounced she would experiment with before they ate.

"I have no personal dresser while we travel," Sabeline sighed, "and Mother will monopolize the maid so."

As the days passed, Rosamund grew to suspect that flattery was all part of Sabeline's calculated persona. Despite Sabeline's youth, Rosamund could hear and see the manner of an experienced woman of court: the theatrical swirl of her skirts as she turned, the teasing smile from underneath an arched eyebrow, the way she threw her head back a little as she laughed, and how she held a goblet of wine with practiced nonchalance. She flirted almost as a habit: sparkling smiles for the men and a laugh at every joke they made. She was just as charming to the ladies, clasping their hands in immediate friendship, whispering confidences to them on all subjects, including confessions of nervousness and uncertainty in what to do and say in various circumstances, a nervousness that, frankly, Rosamund did not believe, for Sabeline was brimming with confidence. Rosamund could not dislike her, but she felt the instinct to keep Sabeline at arm's length regarding any of her own confidences until she could establish the true character underneath the surface allure. She also noted with a slight unease how Milicent seemed most taken with the younger Henry woman. She and Sabeline formed quite the merry pair most evenings, with a chatter and gaiety that Rosamund had seen only too infrequently in Milicent up until now. Occasionally she would catch them looking at her as they conversed, and she could only hope that nothing too unpleasing was being said about her.

Aside from such minor concerns, the time

was spent merrily enough with the new guests. The duchess and her ladies brought a fresh tranche of gossip into the bower, and Lady Aelward did her best to provide similar intrigue to entertain her noble visitors. When the weather was fine, the men hunted on horseback or with falcons. Rosamund was gratified that the duchess also rode, and they spent some pleasant mornings taking sedate rides across the Wold. These were not the headlong gallops Rosamund favored, but she enjoyed the company and the activity nonetheless.

The duchess took a passing interest in Rosamund during these outings.

"You are a pretty girl, my child," she said one day. "Has your father given any thought to when you are to marry?"

"If he has, then I am not aware of a decision upon it," replied Rosamund.

"And how old are you now?"

"Two-and-twenty in the winter."

"Two-and-twenty! Heaven preserve us. Quite ready enough for marriage. I myself was married at the age of fifteen."

"Very good, Your Grace," Rosamund replied neutrally.

"Well, I have a little advice for you, Rosamund," said the duchess, as they paused at the crest of a gentle rise. "It is unlikely your father or your uncle will wait too long before proposing a match for you. You might use your time here at Duloe wisely and pay attention to any young noblemen who pass this way. There is no harm in bringing a man to your relations' attention if you find him pleasing. That is not to say they will find him suitable in their turn, nor that you will be a suitable match for him. There is always rank and fortune to be considered, and you have but a small holding of those. But there is nothing to be lost by exercising what little influence you have before a decision is made for you. What do you say to that?"

"I see the wisdom in your words," said Rosamund truthfully. The duchess was perfectly correct to remind her of what little sway she might have over her marriage, but the conversation depressed her. She did not want to face the truth that she would be married off sooner rather than later, and that she knew not to whom. Neither could she see her way to putting the duchess' advice into practice and asking after any other young men; Alexander Ringewar, for whom she was an unsuitable match in both rank and wealth, had unwittingly seen to that.

"You look dissatisfied, girl," remarked the

duchess. "What were you thinking?"

Rosamund lifted her head and affected a lighter air.

"Only that this might be my last summer here as a maiden."

"Quite so," said the duchess approvingly. "Now, let us continue."

They trotted on across the grass.

Alexander rode out daily during his vigil at Wickford. While the household held its breath over his brother, Lord John, the expectant silence contrasted woefully with the friendly bustle of Duloe, and he found the atmosphere oppressive.

In the third week of his stay, as he rode back along the track to the manor house, he became aware of the distant sounds of hoofbeats, getting closer. Further along the track a rider hove into view. Alexander recognized horse and rider at once and knew it was a messenger from the house. There could only be one reason to send a messenger out to find him.

The gray of dismal rainclouds overhead matched the leaden sensation in his heart as Alexander stepped into Wickford's manor house as its new master. Never would he have sought the title when he knew the cost. His brother had finally succumbed to his injuries in France, and his body was on its way home.

Alexander intended to remain to receive it and bury his brother in the family tomb. Brother, long-cherished friend, adviser, confidante. They had always been close, even with their father so obvious in his favor for his eldest son.

Walking into the main hall, the quietness of the house now overwhelmed him. Memories flooded in; he could almost hear the thundering of his sibling's feet and the shrieks of laughter as they ran and played as youngsters, until their father had threatened to whip them. It was still unconscionable that John would not be returning hale and hearty, with a welcoming smile and firm embrace for his younger brother.

John's wife, Alexander was informed by the housekeeper, was in her chamber attended by her ladies-in-waiting, quite bereft by the news, as she would be for a long time to come, Alexander suspected. They had been a happy couple, from what he had seen. Married only two years, they had yet to bring an heir into the world, but there should have been time for that, time for a child to play here at Wickford under his parents' tender gaze until it was his time to inherit the land as his father had before him.

Alexander thought suddenly of Rosamund rolling down the hill at Duloe castle with Milicent's children, then of other times he had seen her playing with them — showing them how to skim stones in the river, sitting on the ground with her skirts bunched up in her lap, drawing figures in the dust with a stick for them, playing hide-and-seek in the tall grasses of the water meadows — and the way they all laughed with such simple pleasures. There was none of that here, and there should have been. It had not seemed missing before when there was always the promise, the assumption, of John's children to come, but now the absence of such family ties fell heavy upon Alexander's heart.

He would assure John's wife that she could stay at Wickford as long as she wished; he was in no hurry to reside here in her stead. Even then, she would be welcome to stay, though propriety would dictate that she return to her own family in due course. Despite the familiarity of his boyhood home, it all seemed entirely wrong that his brother did not walk here now as its master, but he, Alexander, did. But however he felt, he knew he must do his duty by the estate and by the people who lived and worked upon it.

He had decisions to make.

■ ■ ■ ■

A messenger arrived at Duloe a few days later. A small, private funeral had been held for John Ringewar in the family chapel. Iolanthe was almost in tears for Alexander as she read the short missive.

"Here we have our Robert saved by a miracle," she lamented, "while Alexander loses his brother. It is God's will, but I understand not a bit of it."

Having calmed herself through the afternoon, she reflected on Alexander's misfortune again later in the solar.

"He will have much business to sort out. And he will take it hard. He was fond of his brother. They have always been close, ever since boyhood."

After a pause, Lady Henry spoke. "Perhaps he will now consider marriage," she said to the room at large. "There is now the question of inheritance. For as I understand it, his brother had no heir. Lord Ringewar will inherit all titles and the estate, and then who will it all pass to if he has no heirs?"

Rosamund felt a spurt of anger. Alexander's heart would be broken over his brother's death, while here sat this cold-hearted woman discussing his eligibility as a husband. No matter that Alexander cared not for her; her heart still ached for him if Iolanthe spoke the truth about the magnitude of his loss.

She wondered how long Alexander would remain at Wickford. There was, of course, the distinct possibility that he would not return to Duloe in his capacity as chief man-at-arms now that he had new responsibilities. The thought was a painful one, for in that case he would be as removed from her as if he did not exist.

Fortunately, Rosamund was spared any further irritation at the hands of Lady Henry by the departure of the Marwickshire party for the capital the following day. The castle seemed a quieter place as they resumed their usual routines and pastimes.

"Fret not," said Lord Aelward as his wife complained of how cut off she felt once again from the heart of things. "They will be back again in the blink of an eye, and you can enjoy all the pandemonium of the preparations once more."

Alexander returned three weeks into this peaceful interlude. Rosamund was having a testing morning practicing the viol. She was concentrating so fiercely that it was a good minute or so before she noticed she had an audience listening in the doorway. When she did look up, she nearly jumped out of her seat, for there, in all his glory, stood Alexander.

Having arrived back and been on his way to see Lord Aelward, he had heard the terrible noise and followed it out of morbid curiosity. He could not help but be amused to find Rosamund the culprit, with her face screwed up in a delectable frown. It felt like a long time since anything had made him smile even a little.

"Good morning," he bade her. "No, do carry on." He waved as she made to put down her instrument. "I have a meeting with your uncle presently." But so flustered was Rosamund to see him that she could not put bow back to string, and she instead rose to her feet.

"My Lord," she said, her face serious. "Allow me to tell you how sorry I am to hear of the loss of your brother. It must be a grievous blow."

Alexander looked at her face, the deep sincerity written across it in the wrinkle of her brow and the concern for him in her eyes, and he was touched.

"Thank you," he said gently. "I confess it has been a difficult time."

Rosamund could see the sudden pain

etched in his face.

"I wish there were something I could do," she exclaimed, "but I know there is nothing in the world save time that can ease it."

"Your kindness is deed enough," he replied softly, noting with a grateful surprise how, despite her words, the pain diminished just a little in the presence of her compassion for him. The awkwardness of their last meeting seemed to have faded.

"Have you company at Wickford?" Rosamund asked. "We have all thought of you much since we heard your sad news."

Alexander shook his head. "My sister-by-law and a small party left for her home this week just gone, and I confess I am left alone with my own thoughts too much there. Duloe has much to commend it at this moment on that score."

Once again, Alexander was surprised to find how easily he spoke to Rosamund of his feelings. He had a sudden sense that their shared secrets somehow forged a bond, a belief that what was said to her would go no further. How he knew she had not taken anyone into her confidence he could not fathom, but his instinct was to trust her. Perhaps it was only his loss making him think this way; a natural urge to accept comfort whatever the source. No matter;

her solicitousness was most welcome. He was unexpectedly reluctant to leave her and make his way to Lord Aelward's study. He was still most uncertain what to say to his liege lord regarding whether he ought to relinquish his duties as chief man-at-arms immediately he took up his earldom.

But Lord Aelward was a generous and patient man.

"There is no need to make a decision in haste," he said, clapping Alexander on the shoulder in a kindly gesture of solidarity. "But I do insist you stay for the jousting. I have quite an event planned to see out the summer. It may offer a distraction of sorts, perhaps?"

Lord Aelward referred to his perennial enthusiasm for hosting a jousting tournament each year for any and all knights who cared to participate. Tourneying in times of peace was a hugely popular pastime across the country, and indeed the continent, as well. With confirmation from London that Lord Parnell was safely imprisoned and of little further threat to his neighbors, Lord Aelward considered times stable enough to have already issued an invitation across the realm. Long established and exceedingly popular, the Duloe tournament usually took place before the toil of harvest tied the manor to scythe and plough.

"I must return to Wickford at some point," said Alexander, considering the suggestion, "but for now the estate is in the hands of a capable reeve, and there are no particular problems that force my return. If it please you, I will certainly remain here until the jousting. Then I promise you an answer as to where I consider my duties best fulfilled."

CHAPTER THIRTEEN

The Marwickshires were due back at Duloe, and Iolanthe planned to celebrate her guests' return with a dance. Unlike the riotous May feast, this was to be a formal affair. Fiddles and jigs would make way for the more measured steps of cantigas and caroles. A number of other local nobility were invited for the occasion. Having written the requisite letters during the morning but discovering a lack of sealing wax, Iolanthe sent Rosamund down to the village beekeeper to obtain some more.

Happy to escape the confines of the solar and the tedium of planning the occasion, Rosamund had departed without much attention to the sky. Before she had long left the apiary, the weather performed one of its spectacular about-turns, and the heavens opened. Already halfway home, she decided to hitch up her skirts and keen on for home.

Within a few yards, she was already soaked

to the skin, at which point she realized there was little point hurrying. At least it was not too cold.

She encountered some other unfortunates who had also been caught out by the unpredictable weather: field laborers and a youth shepherding some woolly charges along the castle lane. A lone rider also cantered across from the forest toward the castle hill, with but a cloak for protection from the elements.

Alexander had gambled that the weather would hold for a ride to and from the village smithy for new stirrup irons, and he lost. When he rode across the grass and caught sight of the sopping wet figure of Rosamund, Alexander steered his horse to intercept her path and within a few moments drew up alongside her.

She looked surprised to see him but could not help but laugh as they considered each others' sodden appearance. Alexander offered her his cloak immediately and moved to drape it around her, but she backed away and declined with a smile.

"I am quite soaked through already, and I assure you I am not cold."

"Then allow me to give you a ride back home."

"I am happy to walk; there is no need."

"There is every need in this weather. You will catch a chill."

"Really, I will be quite fine," insisted Rosamund. Tempted though she was, she was uncertain of the appropriateness of accepting.

"And quite obstinate. Very well, I will walk beside you. I cannot simply ride away."

Rosamund hesitated, then capitulated, knowing he would get much wetter himself by waiting for her.

"I do not wish to inconvenience you so in this weather, but I see your mind is made up. Very well, I accept your offer of a ride."

With a nod of satisfaction at the outcome, Alexander offered her a stirrup and his hand to help her up behind him. Despite her skirts she mounted the horse with relative ease. Strength as well as grace, he thought.

As she put her arms around his waist to hold on, the intimacy of Alexander's nearness whirled in Rosamund's head as she felt his strong frame within her arms. She was reminded forcibly of such closeness when they had kissed. She wondered if it was crossing his mind too. As his horse walked along, she had to resist the urge to lay her cheek against his back. Thank goodness he could tell none of this.

"Do you care to canter?" he called over

his shoulder, his voice breaking into her reverie.

"By all means," she called back. It would shorten the thrill of riding with him, but she had no fear of the pace and it would get them out of the rain quicker. Rosamund had to cling more tightly to Alexander, and she had to confess to herself that she savored every moment. It was over too soon. At the stables, Rosamund slipped reluctantly from the horse. She righted her skirts, then paused to wipe rainwater from her face before thanking him.

Looking down at her, Alexander could see rain droplets glistening on the bare skin of her shoulders and décolletage. She was impossibly beautiful, no matter her rain-soaked state.

There was no groom to meet them in the downpour; they had not been seen by anyone in the deserted stable courtyard.

"Proceed indoors out of the rain at once," commanded Alexander, dismounting. "I would escort you, but I must see to my horse."

Regretfully, Rosamund did as she was bade. "Thank you for the ride," she said once again, amazed at how calm her voice sounded in contrast to the turmoil within her.

"My pleasure," he replied simply, and disappeared into the stables.

On her way back to her chamber, Rosamund encountered Maud.

"Rosamund, you are soaked through!" Maud exclaimed. "Why did you not shelter at the village?"

"I did for a good while, but I began to lose hope of when the rain would end," said Rosamund. "It might have continued on for hours. Indeed, it still shows no sign of stopping."

"Let me help you out of those clothes," said Maud, tutting at the bedraggled state of her friend and the dripping trail she had left along the corridor. "Then you may still be lucky and find some food just returned to the kitchens from dinner."

As Maud helped rub her down with linens and found some dry clothes for her, Rosamund kept quiet about her knightly escort home. She decided caution was the better part of valor, and she would wait to see if anybody challenged her at supper on the indiscretion of her ride. She did not think Alexander would mention it to anybody either, keeping his own counsel as he so often seemed to do.

Curling up in bed later that night, the rain

still pattering on the stone outside, she hugged her memories to herself, reliving the ride and the sensation of Alexander so close once again.

A rattle of wheels heralded the return of the Marwickshire party in midafternoon the following day, accompanied by a gusty shower of rain. Peering out of an upper-floor window, Rosamund caught sight of the guests alighting from one of the wagons: the duchess briskly, Lady Henry with a frown of annoyance, and Sabeline with a dazzling smile as though the wet weather were quite the most amusing thing she had encountered that day. Drawing back, Rosamund hurried along to the solar, where she was obliged to wait to greet the arrivals.

To Milicent and Iolanthe's rapture, their visitors were full of the latest news from London. Heedless of the rain that fell outside, they formed an eager audience hanging on the every word of the duchess and Lady Henry as they held forth on the latest intrigues at Court. Their spell was only broken by the announcement of a sumptuous supper for the guests.

Conversation continued in the Great Hall's main anteroom as they waited for Lord Aelward, the duke, and the other men to arrive for supper and facilitate any new introductions. The main one of which, Rosamund realized as the men filed in, would be to introduce Alexander to the Henrys. He had met the Marwickshires before in London but had apparently never chanced to cross paths with Sabeline and Lady Henry.

Rosamund was aware of a stirring unease within her as she watched Sabeline being introduced to Alexander. The rain clouds had finally parted in the last half hour, and Sabeline stood, whether by design or by chance, in a late afternoon shaft of sunlight that pierced the room through its narrow westerly window. The golden glow added an extra beauty to her features as she curtseyed low and smiled with devastating charm at Alexander.

"It is such a pleasure to meet you, Lord Ringewar," she said in dulcet tones. "I have heard nothing but good said of you both here and in London."

Alexander accepted the compliment with an easy grace and asked after the acceptability of their journey.

"Oh, it was perfectly tiresome in the rain to begin with," Sabeline said, and she proceeded to engage him in conversation in her usual sparkling manner. With this final introduction completed, the rest of the room broke into smaller groups to chatter once more. Rosamund noted how with a few small steps Sabeline had already drawn Alexander to one side, clearly intrigued enough by him to consider him immediately worth further individual attention. Alexander, she observed, seemed much as he ever was in conversation, polite and attentive, but Sabeline's skillful annexation of him filled Rosamund with a sense of trepidation. She knew where its root lay, for she was now familiar with it: jealousy. Jealousy of a raven-haired beauty who would not fail to note the physical splendor of a man like Alexander. And who was in a far better position to act upon it.

It soon became clear to Rosamund that she did not have a monopoly on speculation regarding Sabeline and Alexander. The subject came up in the bower one afternoon not a week later. It was a week during which Alexander had been a diligent presence during evening entertainments, and there had been no evening during which he and Sabeline had not conversed amiably. They made a handsome couple to any onlooker's eye.

In the grip of another wet afternoon, Milicent had taken Sabeline to the music room, and Lady Henry was resting. In their absence, talk in the bower had turned to the subject of young noblewomen at court waiting to be wed, and thence to Sabeline's marriage prospects.

"I am surprised Sabeline is not already betrothed," Iolanthe said to the duchess as they sewed.

"Oh, she was," replied the duchess. "To the son of the Earl of Northumberland, last year. It was all arranged and would have been quite the match. Sadly, he suffered an illness this winter and did not recover. He was never the halest, it must be said. There was discussion of marriage to the next brother, but he was already betrothed to a daughter of the Percys of York, and to break it off would have caused some considerable bad feeling. And, naturally, Lady Henry was less inclined to accept the hand of the youngest brother."

"As it now stands," the duchess said quite firmly, "I would not be surprised if Lady Henry has not seen a possibility for her daughter right here at Duloe. I mean, of course, Lord Ringewar. Heaven knows Sabeline has the beauty to capture a duke if she were lucky, but she would do very well with a lord of Alexander's new standing."

Rosamund froze at these words. She had thought as much herself, but to hear her own private fear made word by the duchess was quite another matter. That meant it was likely rather than just possible.

"I thought Lord Ringewar didn't wish to marry," Rosamund blurted out, struggling to hide her disconcertion. "He professes himself married to his duty. He has been that way for ten years, have you not said yourself, Lady Iolanthe?"

The duchess laughed, though whether it was at Rosamund's apparent naïveté or at the ideals Alexander had espoused, Rosamund could not tell.

"Well, quite, my dear. He has had a goodly decade of dedicating himself to his blessed chivalric duty then, has he not? Many a man decides to settle down and marry come his age, many a knight among them. It is the natural way of things. Mayhap he is tired of gallivanting around the country at the beck and call of his king, never spending a month in the same bed."

Rosamund knew what the duchess was going to say next.

"Furthermore, he does now have the responsibility of inheritance to consider, and he would do well to consider it sooner rather than later, for his own brother's situation shows how time waits for no man."

Iolanthe then spoke. "It is true, Rosamund, that he has shown little interest in all matters marital for a long time now. He has always voiced an insistence that his feudal duty comes before all else, for he is an honorable man, as we know. But it is a self-evident fact that marriage is not precluded for knights. And only two nights ago," she added with a gleam in her eye, "I heard that he might at last be coming round to the notion."

This instantly captured the interest of all her companions. Once she was sure of their attention, Iolanthe continued.

"I was speaking to him last night after dinner about the impending marriage of one of his men-at-arms, Sir Geraint, and I jested that Lord Ringewar was unlikely to be the reason for the next gathering of the knights to enjoy wedding festivities, but Lord Ringewar . . ." Here Iolanthe paused for dramatic effect. "Lord Ringewar replied, 'I am not so against it. I have had my eyes opened to the possibility.' " She enunciated every word with enthusiastic emphasis.

"Now what do you think of that?" Iolanthe leaned back in her chair, looking at the rest of her companions knowingly. "And if marriage is on his mind," she continued in jovial tones, "who can blame him for taking the notion that much more seriously when a beautiful maiden such as Sabeline appears? Her mother swears she has entranced half of Court, and to look at the men here at Duloe upon her arrival, well, I can quite believe it." She chuckled, quite oblivious to Rosamund's pain. "Yes, it may be high time Lord Ringewar married. He is past thirty now, and as the Duchess says, there is no surprise to a man looking to settle down at such a time, even before the issue of an heir arises. He could certainly do worse than to marry a Henry. And yes, she is such a pretty creature."

Iolanthe's words were like the twist of a knife in Rosamund's heart. She steeled herself to maintain a polite smile lest she give away her feelings, but nonetheless Alice Gregory noticed her stillness.

"You have stopped sewing, my dear Rosamund. Now, I hope we haven't upset you talking of a marriage for Sabeline and others. It will be your turn before you know it."

Rosamund could only be thankful that Alice had misread the small sign of her unhappiness that she had failed to conceal.

"Oh, I am not unhappy," she insisted with a forced smile. *At least not for the reason you think,* she added silently to herself. "I am in no haste to be married. I am quite satisfied in the life my uncle and aunt provide for me here."

Her aunt chuckled kindly.

"Why, bless you, my dear. And I know you do love it here. Why, we hardly see you in your spare hours for all your walking and riding and playing with the young ones. I shall hate to lose you as my companion, but goodness yes, you shall have your wedding day, and not too many years hence, for I would hardly do your poor parents justice if I were to keep you here for the rest of your days!"

The other ladies laughed, and Rosamund managed to smile along with them. Conversation turned to other connections and possible marriages, but of people Rosamund had little knowledge of. They all sewed on until the duchess excused herself and Lady Iolanthe released the younger women to prepare their toilet for supper.

Well then, thought Rosamund as she departed the bower. *It is as good as agreed.* With Sabeline's beauty, fortune, and position, and Alexander's own words to Iolanthe, there was simply no impediment to what already appeared a natural attraction between the two of them. Perhaps it was for the best, Rosamund thought as she scrubbed her cheeks doubly hard with cold water to repress the tears that threatened to spill. Once Alexander was promised to another, perhaps she could finally begin to heal herself of her futile preoccupation with him.

Chapter Fourteen

Two days later, the sunshine returned to Duloe, allowing its inhabitants a little more freedom. As soon as the ground had dried a little, Iolanthe declared a sortie in order.

"We will picnic in the grounds," she announced. "For though I am not one for the outdoors, heaven knows I am as tired of the sight of these walls as every one of you."

Iolanthe insisted the men join them, and so the following day duly saw a cheerful party of noble men and women strolling across the castle grounds for some exercise and amusements before their outdoor victuals. They were preceded by servants carrying cushions and rugs, food hampers, kegs of ale and wine, and canopies to keep off the sun.

They proceeded to a sward not far from the edge of the forest. It offered the sun for those who wished to enjoy it, while the ladies could stay cooler in the shade. Since the walk from the castle had not been particularly taxing, it was agreed that those of a more vigorous disposition would take a stroll around the meandering paths of the woodland before they ate. Alexander declared he would remain to assist Iolanthe with directions for the arrangement of the picnic. Sabeline also declined to wander and instead chose to sit on the picnic blankets with the duchess and her ladies-in-waiting. Rosamund elected to walk. She had little desire to watch Sabeline flirt with Alexander as she would undoubtedly do.

Since hearing the duchess' and Iolanthe's words, Rosamund had toiled to rise above the jealousy that had entered her soul once again. Irritated with the habitual direction of her thoughts, Rosamund had reminded herself repeatedly of her vow to foster a courteous relationship with Alexander and think no further of any other conjunction with him. This was but one of the many days on which she would be challenged in her resolve, and she must simply become accustomed to it. Her peace of mind demanded it.

The walkers departed, soon stringing out into faster and slower coteries as they made their way under the shaded canopy of trees. Rosamund and Maud started briskly, but

Rosamund was distracted by what she thought was the sight of some wild strawberries.

"I will return forthwith," she said to Maud, before leaving the path to explore. There was no harm in discovering a new patch of succulent summer fruits. By the time she returned successfully with a handkerchief full of the small, seeded berries, she was behind the dawdlers at the tail end of the party. Content with her own company, she was happy to tarry behind awhile, absorbing the tranquillity of her surroundings, until she realized another walker was about to catch up with her. She turned and was surprised to see it was Alexander. In the warmth of the day he had already shed his jerkin. The cool of a linen shirt was all that covered his broad chest, and she could not help but note once again the impressiveness of his physique. How difficult the simple vision of him made it for her to forget her attraction to him and her despondency at his likely intentions toward Sabeline!

He hailed her with a brief wave and soon caught up with her.

"There was little need for my assistance," he said as he approached. "Lady Iolanthe has the business in hand. And a walk encourages the appetite better than a rest upon the grass, I find."

"That was my thought on the matter," agreed Rosamund civilly as they continued on together. She could not seemingly dismiss him from her affections, but she had resolved not to allow her senseless jealousy to mar their cordial relationship. There was a little comfort in it, and certainly more dignity. Nonetheless, she caught herself wondering uncharitably if Sabeline might also have decided to walk if she had known Alexander would elect to do so.

"But you linger behind the others?" Alexander asked, clearly expecting her to be further ahead.

"I spied these." Rosamund lifted her small parcel of pickings and offered him some. He smiled at her, and Rosamund's heart twisted a little.

"You intend some archery?" she asked him, noting the quiver and bow slung over his shoulder.

"Indeed," Alexander replied. "I thought I might sport a little before we eat."

He glanced at Rosamund. "You have some skill with a bow and arrow."

Rosamund was reminded a little uncomfortably of the man she had shot in the forest at Pilning, but she took a look at the bow and replied, "I am a fair shot."

"Only a fair shot? I believe you downplay your talents in the interests of modesty," Alexander said. He seemed in a pleasantly lighthearted mood. Rosamund was pleased for him if a little cheer was possible for him in his bereavement, and she was encouraged to respond in kind.

"The chaplain might remind me that I lack humility if I agree with you too enthusiastically."

"I am not convinced that false modesty is such a virtue," Alexander countered. "Besides, the chaplain is not here to chide. What would you say if proper pride were more the virtue here?" he said, stopping suddenly in the middle of the path. "I am curious, Lady Rosamund. If you were to take my bow and arrow, where would you be confident of hitting your target? The oak there, perhaps?" He pointed to a wide oak tree fifteen yards ahead.

Rosamund's pride, proper or otherwise, was a little offended.

"Why, I could hit that target easily, and further besides," she declared.

Alexander looked at her with his clear green gaze.

"Indeed?" was all that he said.

"You don't believe me," she said, searching his expression and finding a challenge written in the slight curve of his mouth.

"I have said no such thing," he said.

"But you give the impression you doubt me. Very well, I will show you."

"As you wish," he mock bowed, and then she knew he had been leading her to take the bow and show him all along. But she found she was enjoying the unaccustomed banter and took up the challenge.

"What target do you propose?" she asked.

"I leave it to you," he replied.

"Very well," Rosamund repeated, pausing to survey their surroundings. "I choose the elm with the ivy hence." She pointed to a tree thirty yards distant. Alexander raised his eyebrows in mild surprise at the ambitious target but nodded his approval.

With her prowess to prove, she breathed in to steady her nerve. She aimed the bow carefully, pulled back the string and released her arrow. Singing through the air, it hit the trunk dead center.

She broke into a smile of delighted satisfaction.

"Well," said Alexander, also smiling. "It is as I suspected. You have skill with a bow and arrow indeed; that much you have proved. We must add archery to the list of talents you possess: horseriding, nursing, and the viol among them."

His last words made her laugh aloud despite herself, but there was a look of genuine admiration in his eyes as he spoke, and she felt a swell of pride.

"But I must ask," he added. "Where did you learn to shoot?"

"I have three brothers, two of whom undertook knightly service themselves," explained Rosamund. "And my father has instructed pages and squires of his own. I would often ask to practice with them, and they indulged me."

"Hardly an indulgence," said Alexander. "I imagine you might have taught them after some time."

Rosamund smiled at his compliments.

"I am hardly a great archer, but I do like to try. My brothers could mostly outshoot me, and in point of fact my cousin Marianne is a better archer than me."

"Then I would not like to meet your cousin Marianne in battle," said Alexander gallantly. "I acknowledge here and now my admiration for the skill of women archers the land over."

He was teasing her again now, and his humor emboldened her.

"Well then," she said. "You would not consider it beneath you to match me in an archery competition? Here in the forest. For you said you intended some sport."

"Ha!" said Alexander, laughing. "You have me in a fix now. My refusal to meet your challenge would offend you if you thought I did not wish to beat you. But if you think I refused knowing you to be my equal, then it would be a blow to my very honor." He looked at her with amusement. "A clever trap indeed. Therefore I accept, for I must defend my honor against your challenge."

Their eyes gleamed at each other in the enjoyment of being suddenly involved in such a contest, and Rosamund rejoiced in the moment. Once again, they spoke so openly, so easily with one another. Her skill with a bow and arrow gave them common ground on which she was not overwhelmed by her feelings for him. In her new attempt to solicit friendship, she was enjoying sparring with him, and if she were not mistaken, he was enjoying it too. Sometimes, thought Rosamund, he was so impenetrable, and at others like this how wonderfully easy to talk to. These were the times when she knew that it was not just a surface attraction to him that drew her so magnetically, but a deeper emotional pull. Try though she might to deny it, the magic of him still sang in her veins.

Then he was measuring his pace out and taking aim at the tree into which Rosamund's arrow had flown. Quick as a flash his arrow embedded itself in wood barely an inch below her own. He lifted an eyebrow at her.

"Very well," said Rosamund in a considered tone, which belied the spark in her heart. She spun around on one heel, looking for another target. "There," she pointed to the branch of a tree about forty yards from where they were standing. Alexander whistled. "I will not win this contest easily, will I?" he said.

"You may not win it at all," said Rosamund reprovingly.

Despite her retort, again he matched her shot, and their arrows sat side by side in the tree branch. He smiled at her again. Unsettled, she marched off to retrieve all four arrows, so that her face could not betray her. Wresting them from their targets, she turned away from the tree branch to find Alexander behind her.

"So what challenge do you have for me next, Lady Rosamund?" he said softly. Her heart flipped inside her chest. She started back a little, her senses heightened by his closeness.

He held up the empty quiver. "I brought

this for the arrows."

Rosamund quickly gathered her wits. She had been startled by his question, wondering if it had a deeper meaning. But in disappointment she realized he was just assisting her. She took the quiver and was about to thank him when there came a sudden call, and none other than Sabeline appeared through the trees.

"What are you two up to here under the trees with not a chaperone in sight?" she asked archly. Rosamund could not help herself and blushed with embarrassment at Sabeline's insinuating tone.

Alexander showed no such awkwardness. Doubtless because he does not feel any, thought Rosamund, her happy mood deflating rapidly.

"We are engaged in an archery contest," Alexander said, smiling welcomingly at Sabeline. "So far we are an even match."

Rosamund's mood sank further at the easy familiarity between them.

Sabeline gave a lift of her eyebrows as though she didn't believe Rosamund could possibly be evenly matched with Alexander unless he was letting her win. Rosamund was irked.

"Would you care to join us?" she asked rather unfairly, for she knew Sabeline had no skill with a bow and arrow.

Sabeline let out a laugh and rolled her eyes. "As if I would be any use at such masculine pastimes," she trilled, at once both squashing Rosamund's insincere request and managing to discomfit Rosamund for her unfeminine pursuits.

It was foolish to respond with antagonism, Rosamund scolded herself, for even when she did, Sabeline was quite capable of defending herself.

"Lord Ringewar, you neglect the rest of us," purred Sabeline. "My mother insists upon your company and sent me to find you."

Did she indeed, thought Rosamund, disbelievingly.

Alexander clearly felt obliged to return and duly escorted both women back to the picnic copse. For the rest of the outing, Sabeline managed to keep Alexander to herself in conversation, and Rosamund's earlier happiness during the archery contest faded swiftly away.

On the way home, Rosamund was surprised to find Sabeline falling into step beside her. Sabeline engaged in lighthearted colloquy for a little while about the picnic, and Rosamund responded politely. She could not help but wonder if Sabeline had a purpose in approaching her. So it proved.

"I was rather impressed with your archery skills this afternoon," Sabeline said. "I have no such skill myself as you know. And I rather think," she continued, swishing her skirts as she veered around a muddy patch in the grass, "Lord Ringewar was somewhat impressed too." She paused. "He is a handsome man, is he not?"

"Lord Ringewar? Yes, I would say he is," replied Rosamund, truthfully but warily. Was Alexander the subject toward which Sabeline was purposefully headed?

"A little more so than the average, do you not think?" Sabeline suggested.

"That could be said," Rosamund continued cautiously.

"Why, it certainly could." Sabeline skipped over a small fallen tree branch. "And said by you, is my guess."

"I do not recall saying such a thing."

"But you think it, do you not?"

"I agree with you he is a handsome man."

"And quite to your liking," said Sabeline with a little laugh in her voice.

"I am not sure what you mean," Rosamund replied guardedly.

"Oh, I have seen it on your face, my dear." Sabeline's tone was light but with a hint of mockery. "You are a little taken with our handsome Lord Ringewar, are you not?"

"Indeed I am not," retorted Rosamund, but a dull flush had risen on her cheeks.

Sabeline laughed lightly.

"Does she protest a little too strongly?" she asked as if questioning herself. "Why, it is my opinion that she does. But never fear, Rosamund, your secret is safe with me. I am not one to make sport with others' feelings."

Which is exactly what you are doing now, thought Rosamund furiously.

"But I confess I do delight in a little tête-à-tête with another lady on such diverting matters. We will keep it between ourselves, of course," continued Sabeline sweetly. "I understand how you feel, my dear. I have not been immune to the odd infatuation myself and was not always so bold as to talk about it with all and sundry."

"You are quite mistaken in your assumptions," Rosamund said. "I harbor no such feelings for Lord Ringewar. I hardly know him."

"Since when was hardly knowing a man an impediment for finding him pleasing on the eye?" laughed Sabeline in genuine amusement. "It is far more likely the opposite, in my experience.

"But you cannot fool me, my dear," she continued, her tone changing ever so slightly. "As I said, I have been in the grip of such fascinations myself in the past. I see how it takes you. Must I outline the evidence of my eyes? I have seen how you glance at him when there is a chance, though you do not gaze for long. But there is something in the brief flick of an eye that betrays, for if you do not care for the object at which you look, then why not gaze a little longer? As one would look at a mere conversational companion, or a pleasing view? It is the stolen glance that gives us away."

"You are imagining things —" began Rosamund, attempting to keep her temper, but Sabeline cut her off.

"Oh come, Rosamund, do you think I am a fool?"

"Of course not."

"Then why do you not confess it to me?" she giggled brightly. "We could have much sport, you and I. There is no shame in it. I would reveal to you those who have captured my admiration in just such a way in the past."

Rosamund had absolutely no interest in hearing about Sabeline's former infatuations, and she knew that Sabeline's intent was not to share intimacies but to elicit the knowledge she suspected about Rosamund's feelings for Alexander. What Rosamund did not know was why Sabeline desired to know so strongly. She, Rosamund, was hardly a matrimonial threat for Alexander's hand. Keeping her composure as best she could under Sabeline's onslaught, she shrugged her shoulders helplessly.

"Much as I welcome your confidence," Rosamund lied, "I assure you I have nothing of interest to mention on the subject of Lord Ringewar. I have come to a respect for him in the short time I have known him, but that is all."

"As you wish." Sabeline's mouth was friendly but her eyes were cold. "But I am all ears should you ever wish for a confidante."

I would sooner trust Brunhilde to keep my confidence, Rosamund thought. Out loud, she merely said, "You are very kind, but I'm afraid I prove quite a bore when it comes to gossip."

Sabeline smiled a hard little smile but pressed her no further.

Back at the castle, Rosamund was disconcerted. She had done her best to conceal her feelings for Alexander and had thought herself successful. Yet Sabeline had come as close to the truth as anyone and had not seemed convinced by Rosamund's evasion. She had precious little upon which to base her speculations, but despite Rosamund's denial, she had guessed astutely. Rosamund did not know what Sabeline might do next. Was she intending to mention her suspicions to anyone else? Had she already? Since her arrival she had enjoyed Milicent's company most regularly, and Rosamund had no doubt that Milicent would be thrilled to share in any confidences Sabeline might care to bestow upon her, for the glamour of Sabeline's connections had clearly captured her.

Rosamund stiffened her shoulders. She was worrying needlessly. The worst that could happen if her attachment were discovered would be for people to laugh and talk of it awhile. It would be an embarrassment, but not an unbearable one. Why should she expect to be immune from castle gossip? All others were mentioned at one time or another. All the same, the thought of word reaching Alexander himself drew an involuntary grimace from her.

Or perhaps Sabeline merely found it a private amusement to know that Rosamund had feelings for a man whom she, Sabeline, was quite possibly to ensnare for her own before very long.

Iolanthe had noted something else on the subject of Alexander and Sabeline too, and she mentioned it in a discreet moment while Rosamund was helping her plan meals one morning.

"We will have to consider that some of our guests may tarry a little longer; I refer to the Henrys. Their plan was originally to stay here at Duloe but three weeks; instead, there has been mention of five, to include your uncle's tournament." Iolanthe lifted her eyebrows meaningfully. "I can think of only one good reason for women to stay on for a tournament, and it is not on account of their love of jousting."

The following evening was the dance Iolanthe had instigated in honor of her guests' return. The trestle tables had all been moved after supper to allow room for the dancing. The evening light still remained, but myriad candles already burned to provide a blaze of light into the night. The closest nobility, gentry, and knights had traveled through the day to join them and now stood talking together animatedly in all their finery. The noblemen wore jerkins trimmed with fur for the occasion; the women had elaborate headdresses. Serving women and pages circulated among them with trays, offering wine, sweetmeats, and tiny, fruit-filled pastries. Lilting music floated down from the gallery, where the musicians played.

Not long after Rosamund's entrance, a new tune began, introducing the first dance. Lord and Lady Aelward stepped into the center of the room to lead the dancing and were followed by other couples, their fine silks rustling as they took up their positions. Soon the floor was a kaleidoscope of color as the pairs of dancers stepped and swirled in the pattern of the dance.

With no established partner, Rosamund took the time to watch the enchanting sight. So engrossed was she with watching that she only noticed Alexander when he had been standing by her for some moments. He greeted her amiably, and she sank a hurried curtsy to him, but her conversation with Sabeline made her instantly self-conscious about how she responded to him. At all costs she must express no more than a polite interest in him.

"You have not taken to the floor yet," Alexander commented. "I did not think there would be much of the wallflower about you."

Rosamund was just forming a reply when Lady Henry swept up to them with Sabeline in her wake, allowing them no chance to exchange further pleasantries.

"Why, Lord Ringewar," she smiled, ignoring Rosamund entirely. "What a pleasure, I'm sure." She bent in toward him in a faux conspiratorial manner. "You recall promising at dinner last night to partner my daughter, Sabeline, in a dance tonight."

"I recall it well, Lady Henry," Alexander acknowledged.

"Splendid!" beamed Lady Henry, taking a step backward and propelling her daughter smoothly past Rosamund and toward Alexander. "And hark, the next dance begins already. Shall I release you to the floor? There is no need to stand and keep company with me; I shall be quite at my ease."

Sabeline, who could at least have pretended to be embarrassed at such blatant maneuvering, thought Rosamund, showed no such discomfort, and gave Alexander a dazzling smile before dropping her eyes and proffering her hand. Alexander could hardly refuse. *But, of course, why would he want to,* Rosamund reflected, taking in the view of Sabeline's immaculately coiffed black hair and luscious figure, emphasized most flatteringly by a sculpted scarlet gown.

"If you will forgive me, Rosamund," Alexander said, looking over Sabeline's shoulder as he escorted her away. But he seemed all easy charm rather than regret.

"Of course she does, Lord Ringewar," laughed Lady Henry, "and I shall look after her myself, I promise you."

She watched with obvious satisfaction as Alexander led Sabeline to the dance floor.

Alexander danced not one, or even two, but four dances with Sabeline before they forsook the dance floor. Even then, he hovered attentively at her side. Conscious of her desire not to be seen paying too much attention to his whereabouts, as the night wore on Rosamund could still not help but be painfully aware of how they seemed always together whenever she saw them: laughing, drinking, then dancing again. Lady Henry had been right. Spending any time with Rosamund would have been a mere courtesy, a courtesy that Alexander did not in fact seem willing to pay her in any case.

Rosamund's heart was twisting in pain. Finally, she fled the room with as much decorum as possible. Trusting she went unnoticed, she weaved her way along stone corridors and up steps, all the way up to the quiet south battlements, where the cool night air soothed her hot cheeks and she could give way to tears, should they come. Rosamund leaned over the stone parapet. She was steeped in misery. Of what purpose was a dance full of eligible young men when the only man she wanted to dance with was committed to the most beautiful woman in the room? She felt a deep dismay at the turn of events.

You deceived me, Alexander Ringewar, she thought angrily. *I could have borne never having you if your duty had taken you away. I could have borne it if you had never shown the slightest interest in me.* But he had kissed her, their arms wrapped around each other like the tangle of forest branches and creeper that had surrounded them. He had whispered her name like it had meant something to him, and it had moved her. Now he danced in another woman's arms. The wind atop the battlements whipped Rosamund's hair, and she brushed it away from her face furiously. Tears pricked at her eyelids. *No,* she thought; *I have not cried for you before; I will not cry now.* She had indulged in a foolish fantasy, and tonight was nothing but the bleakest of reminders.

CHAPTER FIFTEEN

In contrast to Rosamund's inner despondency, the rest of the castle was buzzing with anticipation of Lord Aelward's tournament. There would be three days of spectacle, entertainment, and carousing. Messengers had been sent out to the capital and to all corners of the country. Happily, the weather had warmed and dried again as knights started arriving and pitching their small tents on the broad sweeps of grass outside the castle and manor house, while their squires hammered wooden poles into the ground to tether their mounts. Lowlier men-at-arms were dispatched to the village to spend their nights there while more noble jousters were accommodated at the castle.

Meanwhile, men from the village were busy raising platforms upon which the castle nobility would sit to watch the tourneying. Some carried poles and planks while others hoisted them into place and hammered in wooden pegs and ropes to secure the edifice. When the men had finished, the castle servants hung bunting and drapery to decorate the platform and provide shelter should the weather turn suddenly inclement. Other men counted out the length of the tournament arena in long strides and pegged rope and flags as markers. The lists along which the contestants would joust were positioned in the center, running parallel to the viewing platform. Lowlier spectators would sit on the grass around the edge of the roped-off field.

The first day of the tournament dawned bright and sunny.

Rosamund sat between Maud and Godith on the erected platform, both of whom were visibly excited after the dramatic spectacle of a number of one-to-one jousts. Rosamund was dismally aware that it was the call to tourney that kept Alexander at Duloe. Now that the tournament had begun, she felt as though her time with him was running out, and it was difficult to raise her spirits in keeping with the atmosphere around her.

As they waited for the next combatants to enter the lists, Maud smiled at Rosamund and gripped her hand in excitement. Rosamund tried to smile back as best she could in response to Maud's good humor, but she was weighed down by the vision of Sabeline a few seats along from her, sitting between Lady Henry and Iolanthe. Sabeline was dressed in an exquisite green robe, her raven hair glossier than ever and her face shining radiantly.

The first of the next two combatants cantered up to the platform to request a token from one of the ladies. He was a young knight, fresh of face, with laughing brown eyes and chestnut brown hair. Rosamund recognized him as Sir Philip, the knight who had asked Maud to dance on the night of the May feast. Bowing as low as he could, he brought his horse to a standstill in front of Maud, who was absolutely delighted to be asked for a token. Beaming assent all over her pretty face, she removed a lace-trimmed cotton handkerchief from her sleeve with trembling hands and tied it around her knight's lance, which he had rested upon the wooden rail of the seating platform.

Maud was even more thrilled when her knight won his joust on the second approach. As he cantered past the stands, he flipped up his visor and wheeled around to face her. He extended his free arm in a bowing gesture and smiled broadly at his sponsor. Maud was enchanted. She could hardly sit still and kept clutching Rosamund's arm and beaming at her long into the preparations for the next joust. Maud's happiness was infectious, and so charmed was Rosamund by Maud's jubilation that she hardly noticed that it was Alexander who now cantered over in his turn. When she saw him, he was already but a couple of yards from the stands, at the end furthest from her. She sobered immediately. He had slowed in front of Sabeline. Of course, she thought miserably, he will ask her for a token; it is only fitting. She cast her eyes away, forcing a bright smile onto her face as though admiring the colorful scene without a care in her head. She did not wish to see the pleasure on Sabeline's face, nor give away her own envy.

She was nudged in the ribs by Maud and turned back toward her. It was then she saw that Alexander had not stopped in front of Sabeline but had brought his horse to an impeccable standstill in front of Rosamund herself. She almost started with surprise, but Alexander was practiced courtesy itself.

"Fair lady Rosamund," he addressed her in the traditional fashion. "Would you bestow a favor upon me to speed me on my way?"

Rosamund could hardly believe what she was hearing, even as her heart soared.

"It would be my pleasure," she replied automatically, hoping her voice did not give away her emotion. As Maud had just done before her, she withdrew a handkerchief from her gown and tied it to his proffered lance. Then she looked up at him again and was struck by the vision of him, by the physical presence of the man who haunted her thoughts daily. He was now her knight for the duration of the competition.

She suddenly remembered to give the customary reply.

"You have my blessing."

"My grateful thanks," he said softly back to her, his green gaze upon her all the while. Then he was gone, flipping down his visor and cantering to the end of the lists.

Rosamund did not dare look at anybody else, so fiercely was she concentrating on concealing the excitement and confusion that had flared within her. In particular, she dared not turn toward Lady Henry and Sabeline for fear of the fury that must surely be directed at her. Yet she had done nothing to invite his attention; he had bestowed it of his own choosing. Maud was beside herself with excitement.

"Now we both sponsor a knight for the jousting," she repeated incessantly.

Rosamund was not surprised when Alexander won his joust on the first approach, for she knew he was an outstanding horseman. It would be a little while now until his turn came to joust again in the next round of the competition. She sat almost incognizant of the competitors who followed, for she was still in some turmoil over his request. After the dance but a few nights ago, she had been utterly convinced that his heart had been captured by Sabeline, for why else had he spent the night so attentive to her? Was it some game, some ploy to influence the negotiations of marriage to Sabeline? That did not seem in Alexander's nature, but Rosamund could think of nothing else. She only dared to turn and look at the Henrys when another knight from a neighboring manor asked for a favor from Sabeline. Sabeline was all smiles as she bestowed one upon him. If she was angry, she hid it well.

Rosamund's heart jumped a little when she finally saw Alexander's blue and gold heraldry return. He cantered easily up to his end of the field, armor gleaming in the sun. This time he took his opponent in two charges.

In the third round, it took three clattering crashes before Alexander managed to unseat the knight he was pitted against. Rosamund's heart was in her mouth on each approach. She gladly accepted a mead from a servant when the round was completed, for it was hot sitting in the sun, even under the canopy, and her mouth was dry.

Now Alexander was due to ride again almost at once, and against the very knight whom Sabeline sponsored. Sabeline made a great show of clapping in support of her knight, as though she had no cares at all about the identity of the opposition. Rosamund was more understated in her applause.

Alexander dispatched the knight in one pass, for his unfortunate challenger had slipped in his stirrup a little on his approach, leaving him off balance. Alexander acknowledged his luck with a wave as squires helped the unseated man back to his feet. Rosamund could not help but look: Sabeline applauded her fallen knight with an expression of sympathy, but as Alexander trotted out of the arena, Sabeline's eyes were upon him.

In the next joust, Maud's knight was also unseated by his opponent, and Maud groaned in disappointment. But she clapped for him until her hands were sore, and for her pains he blew her a kiss as he departed. She was ecstatic.

The final joust was now upon them, Alexander and another lordly knight fighting for the honor of victory.

Their first pass was a chancy affair, neither afflicting a blow upon the other. On their second pass, the other knight caught Alexander a glancing blow and nearly unseated him. The crowd gasped. On the third pass, they both missed again, but on the fourth Alexander lunged forward and seized the advantage. His opponent toppled, and the crowd erupted in cheers.

Rosamund's face was wreathed in smiles of pride and relief; she could not help it. Alexander flicked his visor up and cantered around to the platform. Here, he undid Rosamund's handkerchief and handed it back to her. His own smile revealed his satisfaction in winning.

"You brought me good luck, Lady Rosamund," he said to her, steadying his horse.

"It was a magnificent match," Rosamund exclaimed, her eyes sparkling. "It could not have been more exciting."

Thoroughly overexcited, Alexander's steed reared up. With a laugh, Alexander let the beast have its head. His eyes met Rosamund's once more before he steadied his mount and moved along the platform to receive a winner's cup from Lady Aelward.

Only when Rosamund turned with Maud and Godith to leave the dais did she catch full sight of Lady Henry's unsmiling face.

CHAPTER SIXTEEN

That night, dancing was held once again in the Great Hall, and the lanterns were lit in the grounds. Entering the hall, Rosamund saw Lady Henry making straight for her. Expecting displeasure, she was disconcerted when the woman broke into a delightful smile. She had a young man in tow; Rosamund recognized him as the knight whom Alexander had defeated in the first round of the jousting that afternoon.

"Rosamund, I have an introduction to make," Lady Henry said. "This is Sir Edward Monckton. Since we first spoke tonight, he has been insistent that I introduce him to you. He is the son of Lord Thomas Monckton, the baron. They reside at Florham, some fifteen miles away."

"Yes, I am aware of the name," said Rosamund, as Edward bowed to her.

"May I have the pleasure of your first dance, Lady Rosamund?" he asked, his gaze never leaving her. There was no reason for her to refuse, and she allowed him to escort her away from Lady Henry. Yet her first instinct toward him was one of mild unease. The way his eyes wandered over her body a little too obviously unnerved her. He did not seem to care that she noticed, and his smile verged on a leer as he danced with her.

When the dance ended, Rosamund claimed a desire to sit down, but she could not shake Edward off, for he pretended solicitude and hovered next to her, taking a glass of wine from a passing servant to hand to her. Rosamund thanked him but declined and looked away, offering him a nod of acknowledgement in place of the natural smile she would have offered most others. She supposed he would no doubt think her haughty, but she found herself reluctant to act in a friendlier fashion toward him than was strictly necessary.

To her great relief, her uncle passed by the next moment, humming along with the music. Seeing her sitting there, he exclaimed, "Ah, Rosamund! Your aunt has quite abandoned me to see to some culinary crisis or other. Would you care to dance with an old man?"

Rosamund could not have been happier

to accept and took to the floor again with enthusiasm. She was enjoying her turn with the kindly lord when he turned to wave at a good acquaintance as they passed, and somehow he tripped and fell. Servants helped him quickly to the edge of the room, and Rosamund followed him in concern.

Fortunately, Lord Aelward had suffered no more than a mild twist to the ankle, but he accepted the need to sit gently for a short while. Rosamund had resigned herself to the untimely end to their dance when she heard her uncle saying, "Poor Rosamund, you have lost your partner, such a fool am I. But all is not lost. Hi! Over here, my dear Alexander!"

Rosamund followed his gaze to where Alexander now turned toward them at the sound of his name. He strode over.

"Alexander, would you care to oblige the young lady and finish a dance with her on my behalf?"

"I would stay with you, my Lord, if you have hurt yourself," Rosamund protested.

"Nonsense!" said Lord Aelward, brooking no discussion. "Lord Ringewar will be happy to oblige. Won't you, sir?"

Rosamund heard Alexander's attractive voice reply that it would be a pleasure, and with no choice left to her she looked up at him. Time seemed to slow a little as she met his eyes. He bowed low, and she remembered her manners enough to curtsy in response. She could not help but feel the familiar racing of her pulse as he stood before her once again, towering above her by several inches. His green eyes were piercing, and she had to drop her gaze.

"Would you do me the honor of continuing this dance with me?" he asked as he extended his hand toward her. She braved a glance up at him again and took his hand. Despite Lady Henry's glares and despite everything she had told herself a hundred times about him, she had no thought of refusing.

It was nothing more than courtesy, a suggestion from her uncle, that had led him to ask, but as she held his hand she could feel the smooth, dry warmth of his skin. His fingers closed around hers with a gentle but firm pressure. For that instant she felt as though her whole being were concentrated there where his skin touched hers.

He led her back into the dance, gently propelling her to the end of the row of dancing women while taking a place opposite her in the line of men.

Rosamund didn't know how she managed to remember any steps in the next few minutes. All she could think of was how she was dancing with Alexander after all, of the touch of their hands as they turned gracefully with the other dancers, the brush of his clothes against her as they completed their movements — how, despite her desire to remain detached and look away, time and again their eyes met as they faced one another, because she could not keep her eyes away from him. When the dance finished and he led her cordially back from whence they had come, she could have cried with disappointment when he finally let go of her hand.

"Thank you for the honor," he said, ever the gentleman, but his eyes had a look of intensity in them. "You dance beautifully."

"Thank you, my Lord." She wanted to say how natural it felt to dance with him, how it suffused her with a rush of pleasure that she had never felt with another partner, but of course that was unthinkable.

At that moment, Rosamund became aware of someone at her shoulder. It was Edward Monckton once more. He bowed to them.

"Good evening, Lord Ringewar. May I congratulate you on your day's tourneying? Splendid jousting earlier."

"Sir Monckton, thank you." Alexander gave a bow in response. "Please accept my apologies for your fall."

"Not at all," said Edward jocularly. "But perhaps in compensation you might release this charming young lady into my care for the next dance."

Rosamund was distinctly unenthusiastic about the arrangement.

"Oh, I have danced a little too much already," she said. "I would prefer to sit a while."

"Then sit with me, come," said Edward, undeterred.

There was little Rosamund could object to in the request, and she reluctantly took the hand he offered. Across the room, she saw Milicent watching her with a half-smile upon her face.

Edward led her to edge of the hall, where he stood leaning a fraction closer to her than she felt comfortable with. The wine must have gone to his head, for it was not long before he departed from customary polite conversation and subjected her to a studied, almost insolent gaze.

"You have quite enslaved me, fair Rosamund," he said. "Ever since I laid eyes upon you, two days previously, on my arrival, I have thought you quite the fairest creature."

Rosamund shuddered inside. It crossed her mind for a second how odd it was that one man could fill her with such a sense of longing, while another could do nothing but repel her.

"It was not my intention," she replied. Her body language screamed lack of interest: she turned away from him as far as she could without seeming rude, and she refused to meet his eye. But her short answer and her uninviting pose did not seem to register as a discouragement to Edward.

"Ah, you young ladies would have us believe that," he laughed. "It is all part of your charm."

"If you are implying that I employ dishonesty in my dealings with men, then you are mistaken," said Rosamund, with no attempt to be gracious.

Edward merely laughed again.

"Whatever methods you use, they have certainly worked on me," he continued unabashed.

Rosamund wished dearly that the conversation had not taken such an unwelcome turn. He was not going to be put off in any tactful fashion.

"Would you care to take a turn with me about the grounds?" he asked. Rosamund did not care to in the slightest. In his eyes, her agreement would doubtless be little less than a declaration of affection. She smiled politely but said, "I confess I often feel a little chilled by the evening air."

"Then allow me to get you a shawl. Wait here." He darted off in search of a servant to send to Rosamund's room. It was his mistake, for Rosamund took the opportunity to depart in haste. Weaving through the merrymakers, she slipped out of the hall through a side door and into a passageway, planning to wait five minutes or so until poor Edward gave up an initial search of the hall for her and fell into new conversation. She had no wish to avoid the party, but even less desire to be courted by Edward Monckton. He was a persistent nuisance. She would be lucky to avoid him for the rest of the evening, but she would do her best to try. She took a quick look over her shoulder, checking to make sure she had not been spotted.

"Avoiding someone?" asked a voice. Rosamund started in surprise. It was Alexander again. As usual, his presence threatened to bring a flush to her cheeks, but this time it was one of guilt.

"You surprised me, Lord Ringewar," she responded, avoiding the question.

"My apologies," he said mildly, but he sounded amused.

"I was merely bowing out of the proceedings for a short time," Rosamund lied. "The noise can get a little overwhelming."

"It surprises me that you need to retreat so soon from a little merrymaking."

Rosamund could tell that Alexander was not fooled for an instant.

"I saw your expression as you were talking to young Monckton," he continued. "I take it his conversation holds no interest for you."

Rosamund was embarrassed on behalf of Edward but admitted reluctantly, "He wanted me to take a turn with him around the grounds. I was not in the mood."

"You are very generous." Alexander grinned. "I have spoken to the man myself, and I cannot imagine he would have much to say that would not bore you or irk you."

What conversation *did* Alexander think would be of interest to her, Rosamund wondered for a brief moment.

"He is not the worst of men by my knowledge, but his interchanges with women would be done considerable service were he to study the chivalric code even for an hour," Alexander continued. Rosamund said nothing at this, but she couldn't help but agree. She was impressed by Alexander's appraisal of Edward's character.

"And what was your excuse for not walking with him?" Alexander asked, teasingly refusing to let her off the hook.

"I thought it a little too cold for my liking," she confessed. She saw laughter jump into his eyes.

"If he knew you better, he would know that was a fabrication and take his leave. I imagine he insisted on finding you a shawl instead," he said sardonically.

Rosamund laughed out loud. "Why, he did!" she exclaimed. Alexander joined in her merriment with his own shout of laughter.

At that moment, Edward appeared in the doorway.

"Why, I thought I had lost you completely, Lady Rosamund," he declared. "But I vowed I would not rest until my search for you was a success."

Rosamund glanced at Alexander and caught a look of mutual understanding in his eyes. Edward turned to Alexander and bowed.

"Thank you for entertaining this delightful creature in my absence," he said. "Will you forgive me if I now borrow her for the walk I promised her in the gardens?"

Rosamund waited gloomily for Alexander's polite assent. Her heart sank at the prospect of enduring yet more of Sir Edward's company. Instead she was startled to hear Alexander say, "With great regret I cannot do so. It was but a half hour ago that I promised the very same to her, and I would feel I had disobliged her greatly by making another man do my own duty."

Edward blinked in surprise as Alexander reached across and offered his arm to Rosamund. She took it reflexively, not knowing quite what to say to the spurned Edward and instead letting her silence masquerade as implicit confirmation of Alexander's statement. Alexander started to lead her down the passageway, then paused.

"The shawl," he said, gesturing at the garment over Edward's arm. "Might I borrow it for the lady?"

"Er — but of course," stammered poor Sir Edward.

"My grateful thanks, sir," said Alexander, nodding his head politely. "Well then, until later."

"Until later," said Edward faintly.

Rosamund managed to keep a straight face until they were along the corridor and out to the gardens. Then she could hold in her mirth no longer. She burst into peals of laughter. Alexander was smiling broadly, and then he too let out a deep chuckle.

Rosamund tried to silence herself with her free hand. Still brimming with laughter, she turned to Alexander.

"I am sorry, but his face . . ." She collapsed into giggles again, and Alexander laughed with her. Eventually she managed to control herself.

"Thank you," she said. "For rescuing me so inventively. I am most obliged."

"My pleasure," Alexander said warmly. "And after all," he said, taking her arm once again and leading her across the courtyard to where others promenaded on the grass outside the castle's walls, "it is my sworn duty to protect those in need."

She laughed again. She was aware of how deeply attracted to this version of Alexander she was, this man of smiles and laughter. Her ache for him was no less than before, but sharing a happy moment with him once again filled her with pleasure.

Just as he had promised, he continued to walk with her.

"I will not hold you to the charade," she insisted, but he shook his head, simply saying, "It is a fine night for a walk."

It was a fine night. The sky was clear of cloud, and stars twinkled above their heads. The moon was full and hung just above the horizon. They could hear the chirrup of crickets in the grass and the distant calls of creatures in the forest, their own dramas unfolding in the dark.

"Lady Rosamund," Alexander suddenly began in a serious tone. But before he could continue he was interrupted by loud whoops. Two young knights on horseback, probably the worse for ale, were approaching. They were throwing a jester's hat to one another as they cantered. As they saw Alexander and Rosamund they called a greeting then cantered around them in a circle.

"Sir Nicholas, jouster extraordinaire," the first introduced himself, doffing his ridiculous hat. "And my companion, Sir Richard.

"Kind lady," he addressed Rosamund, merrily but drunkenly. "We are at your disposal. Set us a task and we shall do your bidding."

They were simply having fun, and Rosamund had no compunction in humoring them.

"Very well," she said. "Lay down your magnificent hat on the ground, good Sir Nicholas, and I would like to know which of you can ride by and lean the lowest to retrieve it while remaining in your saddle."

"Aha!" cried the second rider. "A noble task indeed. Lay down the hat, Sir Nicholas," he ordered his friend.

Sir Nicholas threw it to the ground with a drunken flourish.

"Have at it, brave Sir Richard."

Sir Richard had the first attempt but failed to reach it. Moreover, the amount of ale he had consumed had him struggling gainfully to get back into his saddle, and he hung sideways for a good few moments until finding the strength to haul himself back up. Both knights were laughing, and Rosamund could not help giggling herself.

"A feeble attempt, Richard," Nicholas called. "But look while a true knight completes the task." He rounded on the hat and got a hand to it to grasp it but tumbled from his horse with a mock cry of disaster. Lying on the ground, he called out to his horse, which shook its head and trotted off. "For shame, noble steed," he cried. "You have let me down unconscionably."

Rosamund laughed and shook her head but ran to collect his errant horse. She led it back and patted its nose while Alexander helped up his fellow knight.

"Ale is a vexation to a questing knight," he commented sympathetically.

"Indeed. But I shall show it who is master yet tonight," determined Nicholas. They helped him back onto his horse and handed him his hat.

"My grateful thanks, fair lady and kind sir," he acknowledged. Then whooping again, both men set off back toward the castle at a canter, Sir Nicholas nearly unseating himself again as he turned to wave a farewell.

Rosamund could not help but laugh once again at their comedy. Suddenly checking herself, she wondered if Alexander would think her gauche to laugh at their clowning, or worse, think she had been flirting with them. But he was smiling at her.

"You are even more beautiful when you laugh," he said softly.

She was swiftly sobered by his words and her laughter subsided. A tension sprang up between them. If she let herself believe it, she could see affection in his eyes. She did not know what to say in return. A mere thank-you did not seem appropriate. She was not used to accepting compliments from men, and she was thrown off balance by this one. "I do not know what to say, sir," she admitted, dropping her gaze. "Except thank you, and that there is no need to flatter me."

"I do not flatter you," he said, his voice more forceful. Then more gently, he put a hand to her cheek, tilting her face toward him, as if to study it. Mesmerized, she did not pull away, but looked up at him once again. If her face were an open book of her feelings, then there was nothing she could do about it but let him read it. His own face was moonlit in profile, showing his strong, unsmiling countenance. A muscle twitched in his cheek. They remained motionless for only a moment, then he suddenly removed his hand and offered her his arm.

"Come. Let me take you back to the castle." As they made their way, he did not speak. Rosamund could not break the silence either. She still did not know what it was he had been going to say to her before the knights had interrupted them, but he did not say anything further. When they reached the great hall again, he turned and bowed to her.

"I have monopolized you too long," he said. "My grateful thanks for your company." With that, he turned on his heel and was gone.

It was as much control as Alexander could muster not to kiss Rosamund on the moonlit sweep of lawn. When he had seen her in the hall at the beginning of the dance, he could not help but be pleased. She looked as lovely as ever, dressed in a silk evening gown, with her hair pinned back and a small headdress for the occasion. He had sighted her again as she had left the hall, her intent to escape obvious as she glanced over her shoulder and disappeared into the passageway where he had found her. He wanted to smile at her spirit in escaping from unwanted company but had not wished to offend her by laughing, especially when he realized her pursuer. He was a little sorry to play such a game on poor Edward Monckton, but the man was a fool; mostly harmless, but with an undesirable opinion on women that could only come from not caring to know them as well as he ought.

Turning to thoughts of Rosamund herself, it seemed that she revealed something more of herself every time he encountered her, and each attribute only showed her in an ever better light. This time it was her good humor. He caught himself standing back to observe as she laughed with the drunken knights at their sporting. She was not too shy or too proud to jest with them, and he liked her for it. He watched her smiling face bathed by the moonlight and the glow of the castle fires; there was no doubt that she was a beauty. After his confusion, Edward Monckton would be angry that he, Alexander, had stolen her away for this walk. It was only with a huge effort of will that he had forborne to kiss her again as he had done in the forest clearing. But, Lord help him, he was not going to commit the same offense again. He removed his hand from her cheek and avoided her eyes before he betrayed himself. In his hand's place he quickly offered the cool alternative of his arm and started to escort her back to the castle courtyard. Once again he wondered what her feelings were. He had thought more often than he cared to about the warmth in her eyes when she looked at him. But as Rosamund didn't display any of the obvious flirtations he had seen other women use, he declined to draw a conclusion that she harbored any special feeling for him. No, she had not resisted when he had kissed her, but she had looked a little shocked when they parted, that was for certain, and that was plenty to deter him. He had already chided himself enough for falling prey to his passions like that without needing to do so again. He bid her a curter goodbye than he had intended and left her as quickly as he could. *To ale and song,* he thought, *for all she does is undermine my every desire to merely do my duty.*

CHAPTER SEVENTEEN

Rosamund's head was still spinning with the words he had said to her: *You are even more beautiful when you laugh.* But then his mood had become distant and forbidding as he had taken his leave of her. It was all she could think of as she sat in one of the castle's small gardens alone the next morning, preparing flowers in a press. She was so little experienced in such matters, but everything Alexander had said in the past few days, combined with the way he looked at her, gave her the impression that he had feelings for her. And yet everyone seemed so certain of his imminent engagement to Sabeline. None of it made sense.

She was still pondering Alexander's behavior when someone came into sight around the corner. She was distinctly ungratified to see it was Edward Monckton. It was poor luck to encounter him in such a place, and it made her wonder if he had intentionally sought her out. He approached with a jovial wave.

"Splendid morning," he called. "Perfect for the day's tourneying, do you not think?"

Rosamund summoned up a perfunctory smile.

"Indeed," she offered in half-hearted response.

"What are you engaged in?" Edward asked, approaching a little too closely to peer over her shoulder.

"I press some flowers, to make a dried arrangement with them anon."

"Well, if it is not too impertinent to say it, you are quite the prettiest flower in the garden this present morning," said Edward.

The bluntness of such a sudden romantic overture left Rosamund cold.

"You flatter me," she said, with no hint of warmth, and continued arranging the flowers between the boards of the press, studiously avoiding his eye.

"Only words well deserved," he replied, and when she said no more, added, "Come, do you have no words of encouragement in exchange?"

Deeply uncomfortable, Rosamund closed the press and rose to her feet, clutching it in front of her.

"I am near finished with these flowers and

must return inside. Would you excuse me, sir?"

"I might, if you have no objection to my asking you for a favor at the jousting today."

"You may do as you wish, sir."

"May I, now?" Edward replied, his tone changed in a manner Rosamund instinctively disliked. He looked at her searchingly.

"I may do just that, for I am inspired to action these past two days. You see, I have quite fallen for you, Rosamund Galleia."

Already perturbed by his presence, Rosamund was dismayed by his proclamation. She gave an embarrassed laugh and refused to meet his eyes, even as he shifted his head to try and catch her gaze. She shifted uncomfortably.

"I do not know what to say, sir. I am flattered, but I had no intention to inspire such feelings in you."

"Well that is as may be," he replied. "I think some of you ladies are the very devil, with your plans to capture hearts but your protestations of innocence, but it doesn't matter to me. You have succeeded very well either way. You're quite a beauty, little Rosamund."

He stepped in closer. "You wouldn't furnish an admirer with a kiss, would you?"

He moved in to do so. Alarmed, Rosamund was too quick for him. Still, he persisted, catching her arms and bending in toward her. They tussled for a moment, after which Rosamund wrested one of her arms out of his grip and, almost without thinking, struck him hard across the face with her free hand.

There was a pause while they both stood shocked. Then Edward released her, laughing and smoothing down his robe.

"Upon my word," he said. "You have spirit in you, that's for certain. And I admire your virtue . . ."

But she was already stalking away, distancing herself from the violation of his touch. As she reached the end of the garden and rounded the corner she broke into a run. Where she could run to and feel safe while he remained at the castle she had no idea.

The second day's jousting proved as entertaining as the first. Rosamund was asked for a token by neither Edward nor Alexander, for another knight requested one first and there was no reason for her to refuse. Rosamund saw little of Alexander save through his visor, but she noted with curiosity and a stab of relief that he asked no one else for a token. She had expected him to ask Sabeline, but perhaps he had been thwarted, for another jouster, competing earlier, had asked her for such a token, and she had accepted with the same diligence to courtesy that Rosamund had.

The finale to the day was a mêlée in which numerous knights and their chargers pitched a mock battle. The noise and confusion was of such force that Iolanthe hid her eyes behind her hands, declaring, "They will all kill themselves, and such utter pointlessness when they are truly friend not foe!"

It would solve all my problems quite neatly if they did, thought Rosamund, sighing to herself.

The second night of the tournament also offered Rosamund a reprieve from Sir Monckton's attentions — and Alexander's, she reflected with considerably more regret — for Lord Aelward deemed a feast for the knightly brotherhood only.

The next morning, Rosamund resolved to remain in the company of others at all times to avoid a similarly unpleasant encounter as that of the previous morning. Thankfully, she had had no further dealings with Monckton save for seeing him toppled early yet again in the jousting, but the previous day's incident with him in the garden was still preying upon her mind. She hoped she had deterred him from further interest in her, but nonetheless she could not help but wonder if the encounter would have any further consequences for her.

As it transpired, Maud ran a fever with sickness all that night and on into the third day, and she begged for Rosamund to be allowed to stay and care for her.

"Too much sun, mayhap, sitting at the jousting all day," was the verdict of the physic, contemplating Maud's pale complexion and blond curls. Cheered by a diagnosis that augured an unblemished recovery, Rosamund was nevertheless glad for the excuse to hide away in the women's quarters for the rest of the day. She did not even mind too much missing the dancing in the evening for, in her genuine concern for Maud, she could not have enjoyed herself while her friend lay lonely and fevered in their room. As she and Alice sat in turn with Maud, Rosamund's thoughts turned again and again to the moment at which Alexander had asked her for a token and to the magic of the moonlit walk they had taken.

Rosamund had attempted to put Edward Monckton's unpleasant handling of her out of her mind, but when she was summoned to her uncle's study several days after the tournament's end and the departure of its participants, her first fear was still that the incident with Monckton had occasioned it. She could not help but think scathingly of a man who would complain to another about a woman's behavior in order to cause trouble for her, but from what little she knew of him it would not surprise her. Thus she went prepared to be scolded on grounds of whatever displeasure she had caused him.

As she approached Lord Aelward's study, Rosamund knocked on the thick oak doors and heard a call from within to enter. Lord Aelward was seated at his desk by the far window.

"Ah, my dear." He gestured to Rosamund to sit down in one of the chairs opposite him. Then he beamed at her, and her first thought was that her uncle did not wear the countenance of a man about to chastise her for unseemly behavior.

Lord Aelward spoke. "I have some exciting news for you."

Rosamund raised her eyebrows questioningly, uncertain of what to expect. "Indeed, my Lord?"

Lord Aelward continued. "I have received a letter from your father, who is in good health, you will be pleased to hear, as are the rest of your family."

"I am delighted to hear it," replied Rosamund.

"But he encloses a letter that was sent to him from Sir Edward Monckton. You are acquainted with Sir Monckton, yes?"

"Yes, my Lord. I met him during the tournament." Rosamund said nothing further, until she could glean a better idea of where her uncle was leading.

"Very good. Well, it says here in this letter that Sir Monckton was delighted to make your acquaintance. Now how about this, Rosamund? It seems you must have made a great impression upon him during his stay. He writes of your charm and your beauty — quite so, quite so." Her uncle ruffled the pages of the letters to find the next relevant point. "He goes into some detail about his estate and his worth — he is a wealthy man, I can assure you, Rosamund."

Suddenly, Rosamund had a strong sense of what was to come next but her anticipation was not enough to take the shock out of her uncle's words.

"Suffice to say, Sir Monckton has made you an offer of marriage. My dear, we could see you wed by the end of the year."

Rosamund sat at the end of her bed, a leaden feeling in her stomach. She had absolutely no desire to marry Sir Monckton. Her worst fears were coming true with a rapidity that stunned her. She was to be married off to somebody she positively disliked. There was little chance of saying no. He was a good match for her, if one looked at it with a logical eye. Lord and Lady Aelward were clearly not unduly concerned about him as a husband for her; her own parents would be no more so. There was only her own personal preference, which screamed out that he was utterly the wrong man for her, and that of course was worth nothing.

She had protested to her aunt that she had only been at Duloe for a matter of months: she had understood she was to stay for a year.

"Well, that was originally so, yes," Iolanthe had agreed. "But to receive a proposal of such quality so quickly is quite something. While I was quite dedicated to your education, of course, clearly I need do little more as far as Lord Monckton is concerned. He thinks you are a delight already, which you are, my dear, you are. And you mustn't forget that you are older than many other ladies-in-waiting, so it is no bad thing to receive an offer so quickly. Look at poor Godith, long past your age and never once an offer."

"But I don't wish to be married yet." Ordinarily Rosamund would not reveal her deep ambivalence for marriage, but she had nothing to lose.

"Don't wish to be married yet?" Iolanthe was surprised. "What would be the advantage of waiting?"

Rosamund left the question unanswered. She could not say what she was thinking, and Iolanthe was not, in truth, expecting an answer, so natural was the idea of marriage in her mind.

Iolanthe gave Rosamund a little hug.

"Why, you're just nervous, I believe. Quite understandably, dear. It is a big change, I know, and so soon after coming here. But it is wonderful news; you should be happy. Lady of the Manor! Does that not have a fine ring to it?" Iolanthe was already imagining the ceremony and the celebrations, Rosamund could tell. She felt a deep despair. While her aunt was sensitive in some ways, she was a closed book on this matter. She had no sense that Rosamund could object to marriage itself, and she had no thought of questioning her husband's acceptance of Monckton once the marriage had been agreed upon. She trusted the decision of her own husband, in whose eyes

Monckton was essentially decent: a little boring in his tendency to monopolize a conversation, a little boorish after too much wine, but with no obvious defects that made him fear for Rosamund's welfare. If only Alexander would talk to Lord and Lady Aelward, she wished fervently, for his poor regard for Monckton might have a small influence on them. But there was no reason for her uncle to consult his chief man-at-arms on such a matter. Alexander's opinion would go unknown, and her own unheard.

The news of Rosamund's engagement took Alexander by surprise. He could not prevent a start of concern when he was told by Milicent who the prospective groom would be.

"I suppose you have heard the news," Milicent had said sweetly to Alexander after dinner on the evening of Rosamund's interview with her uncle.

"To which news do you refer?" Alexander asked.

When Milicent told him, he could not help a frown cross his face. He did not reply for a moment.

"It does not seem a match to her liking," he said when he finally spoke.

Milicent laughed gaily. "It is hardly a matter to be decided by her liking," she said.

"But it is a marriage of eminent suitability for her, which is to any woman's pleasure. Besides," she added, noting Alexander's expression, "she is most excited by the proposal. While it is not of much interest to you, I am sure, being a knight with more important matters upon his mind, I do have quite some confidence with her and she has given me every impression that she is by no means indifferent to his attentions, even though it is but a short time since they met. It is not a match without some fledgling affection, I can assure you."

Alexander paused. "Well, it would seem I am in error," he said benignly. When he excused himself shortly afterwards, Milicent released him graciously and turned nonchalantly to converse with Sabeline.

So Rosamund was to be engaged very shortly, thought Alexander. He was extremely reluctant to dwell upon the emotions the news engendered in him, but he was most surprised by the revelation that her intended was Edward Monckton. Together they had laughed about him as they strolled in the castle grounds on the final night of the tournament. She had seemed to take him no more seriously than Alexander himself could take the man. He was puzzled. Of course Lord Aelward and Rosamund's father would have been paramount in making the decision. But Milicent had told him quite openly that she believed Rosamund had feelings for Edward.

He knew Rosamund had gone to some effort to avoid Edward at the tournament, but she had apparently also given him an impression of such fondness that he now considered her for his bride. What did that reveal of her character that he, Alexander, had hitherto unsuspected? Could the proposal really have come with such swiftness, or had Rosamund previously been aware of the possibility of marriage to Monckton? If the latter, it would force him to view her in a different light, and a less flattering one at that. More than he had realized, he now needed reasons to think less well of her if he were to cast her out of his mind, as he must do if she were engaged to another.

A week after the news of Rosamund's engagement, the Henrys were due to leave Duloe and return home. No longer under the wing of the Marwickshires, Lord Henry had sent a wagon and escort for his wife and daughter, and a messenger had arrived giving notice of the escort's arrival two days hence. The messenger also brought a letter for Lady Henry from her husband. No sooner had she read it than Lady Henry sought an audience with Alexander. Inviting him to a private meeting in Lord Aelward's study, she came straight to the point.

"Lord Ringewar, you will know that my daughter's welfare is the issue closest to my heart, as is the case with any mother. She will be nineteen in the autumn, and it is Lord Henry's judgment and my own that she is ready to wed. You are aware of our circumstances and that Sabeline brings a very respectable dowry to her future husband, not to mention being a young lady of title."

Alexander nodded his head in acknowledgment. "Your daughter offers any man a very worthy marital alliance," he replied.

"Quite so," Lady Henry agreed. "And it was with that in mind that I wrote to my husband recently to discuss the matter. Our stay here at Duloe has been a particularly pleasant one." Here a more meaningful tone entered Lady Henry's voice. "I have noted my daughter's enjoyment of your company in particular, Lord Ringewar. And I am hoping I am not mistaken in thinking the affection a mutual one." She paused, leaving an opening for Alexander to respond.

"I have certainly enjoyed Lady Sabeline's

company," he replied truthfully, but when he added nothing further, Lady Henry spoke again.

"In response to my letter, I heard word today from my husband on this matter, and he is most amenable to what I propose to you now."

Alexander suddenly had no doubt what the older woman was going to say.

"We are due to depart Duloe in two days," Lady Henry stated. "Therefore, Lord Ringewar, I must speak plainly. Are you going to ask for my daughter's hand in marriage?"

When the news of Alexander and Sabeline's engagement was revealed the next morning, Rosamund was almost beside herself with misery. She had been expecting it, she told herself. It should have been no surprise and yet the pain of it still shocked her.

When she did not appear in the bower in the afternoon, Maud was eventually dispatched by Milicent to find and fetch her. She found Rosamund sitting immobile on her bed, staring out of the window unseeingly. She noticed Rosamund's tear-streaked cheeks immediately.

"Why, whatever is wrong?" she asked, sitting down beside Rosamund and placing a gentle arm around her shoulders.

When Rosamund did not reply, she questioned her hesitantly. "Is it your engagement? I know you are unhappy about it, that much you have said."

She squeezed Rosamund's shoulders gently. "Edward may yet turn out to be a decent husband."

When Rosamund still said nothing, Maud sighed in sympathy. "It is everything we fear for ourselves, I know, to be entrusted to a man of whom we know so little. I wish I had some words of comfort from my own experience, but I have none. I only know I will be thinking of you every day and will write as often as a messenger goes your way."

Touched by Maud's words, Rosamund reached over to clasp her friend's hand. In the face of kindness, the urge to unburden herself was too strong.

"You are right; my engagement is not to my liking. But it is not simply that."

"Then what else?" asked Maud.

Rosamund hesitated but, taking a deep breath, she finally admitted the source of her now unrelenting sadness.

"I love someone else," she said, and as she spoke her tears started to flow once more.

"Heavens!" exclaimed Maud, looking at her with concern but now also not a little curiosity. "Who? You have never breathed a word about a suitor before now."

"He is no suitor," said Rosamund cheerlessly. "We have no understanding, and there was never any chance of one. Indeed, he is even engaged to another as we speak. I have been such a fool."

"I had no sense of this." Maud stroked Rosamund's hair softly. "Why did you not tell me any of this?"

"I cannot say. You must forgive me that I did not. But you must see it has all been a silly imagining on my part, not worth wasting anyone's time over. Least of all my own." She sniffed and released Maud's hand to wipe her face with a handkerchief.

"But who is it who has set you to such unhappiness?" repeated Maud.

Rosamund sighed heavily. "It is Lord Ringewar."

"Lord Ringewar?" Maud put her hands to her cheeks in surprise. "Heavens! But he is engaged to Sabeline!"

"Quite," Rosamund said grimly.

"Oh, but I did not mean to be so thoughtless," said Maud, chagrined. "But this is all new to me. I knew not that you harbored any special affection for him. Possibly I thought the reverse," she added on reflection, "for I have noted the odd occasion on which you have avoided his company."

"I have misled everyone sorely," Rosamund confessed. "It is true I did not like him overly upon first acquaintance. So stern and always taking himself so seriously. But there were occasions when we talked, and I felt there was an understanding between us. I grew to like him. And try as I might, I have never been able to ignore his countenance, just like others before me. It is piteously weak of me." She started crying again before confessing the worst of it to Maud.

"And he kissed me," she sobbed, covering her face with her hands.

"He kissed you?" Maud was agape. "When?"

"When we went to find the agrimony for Lord Robert. In the forest, after we were attacked."

"Heavens!" repeated Maud. "And then he said nothing more?"

"No, we did speak," admitted Rosamund. "He apologized. Clearly he thought it a mistake. Naturally, what could I do but agree?" She sighed heavily again. "I tried to think nothing of him after that. But after he lost his brother, whenever we talked, he was kind. I resolved on a cordial acquaintance with him once again, nothing more. But I have been undermined in that resolution on more than one occasion. When we danced before the tournament, and when he asked me for a token —" Rosamund stopped abruptly. "But why do I speak of all this? His actions have signified nothing. It is my own imaginings that have led me to such a pass."

"Not at all," insisted Maud, righteous on her friend's behalf. "You surely could not have come to such a notion unless there was some encouragement on his part. And for him to kiss you! It is hardly an action of no significance."

"No, it has all been foolishness," sniffed Rosamund. "As if I have ever been in a position to entertain notions concerning an earl's son. And after the death of his brother — well, if he were not entirely out of my reach before, then that sealed it."

"It is not unheard of," said Maud consideringly. "Your aunt achieved as much."

"They were extraordinary circumstances." Rosamund shook her head. "I am but the daughter of a baron with no favors at his disposal. And now we have the proof of it." She gave a humorless laugh. "Alexander is engaged to Sabeline Henry, exactly as has been predicted since they met. And I have a proposal from a buffoon whom I cannot abide. Oh, Maud, I cannot bear to think of it. I am to marry a man I have no feelings for, and I have lost my heart entirely to another."

She started weeping again. Maud cradled her in her arms, with no idea how to comfort her.

The next day the Henrys departed from Duloe. They climbed into their wagon, full of regretful sentiments at leaving but they wore satisfied smiles upon their faces. Rosamund knew she was not imagining the hint of triumph in Sabeline's eyes as she sparkled at the small group who had assembled to bid them farewell. And who could blame her for feeling triumphant? She had captured the hand of a new earl, and that was no trifling achievement for a woman.

Sabeline had made eyes at Alexander as she peeked out from the wagon one final time.

"Until we next meet," she said, her lyrical voice full of promise.

CHAPTER EIGHTEEN

As the Henrys departed, Alexander had stayed on the forecourt until the wagon had trundled out of sight. He could still not imagine the woman he had just waved good-bye to as his wife. But that was the agreement he had made.

Lady Henry had suggested a wedding at Wickford. Alexander had surprised himself with the swiftness of his refusal, and Lady Henry's eyes had widened a fraction. He had quickly suggested London as more convenient for the bride's family and of no particular inconvenience for him. Lady Henry agreed after momentary hesitation, questioning his reluctance to wed at his own ancestral home, but finding nothing unto-ward with his own suggestion. London would be easier if she and her daughter were to have full influence over the marriage plans. He had stated what he thought was a reasonable monetary sum and agreed that

Lady Henry might plan the celebrations as she saw fit. She had seemed more than happy with the financial latitude allowed to her, and no doubt the Henrys' journey would be filled with happy anticipation over how best to spend it.

It had not been an easy decision, Alexander reflected. He did not love Sabeline. But she was charming, intelligent, and beautiful. She was from a powerful family that was keen to make a connection with his. The alliance would help to protect his manor, and he also had in the forefront of his mind his duty to consider his title's succession. For those reasons, rather than his own personal preference, he had decided to accept Lady Henry's proposal. But deep in his heart he knew there was another reason that had propelled him to such a decision.

The morning of Rosamund's own departure dawned. Looking at Rosamund's strained, unhappy face as she packed a few personal belongings for herself, Iolanthe had remonstrated gently with her.

"You go to your new home to prepare for your wedding day, child. Have you not a little more cheer on such a momentous occasion?"

Rosamund stood in the middle of the

room and turned to face her aunt. She felt no cheer and would not feign it any longer, for there was nothing to gain by doing so.

"I do not wish it," she said bluntly. "I cannot pretend otherwise."

"Rosamund," her aunt chided. "Your father and your uncle both wish this union to happen. Lord Monckton wishes it to happen. What else would you do if you were to refuse this marriage?"

"I accept I have no choice in the matter," Rosamund said disagreeably. "And I have refused nothing."

Iolanthe was too surprised to chastise her niece for her cheek.

"We cannot keep you here forever, Rosamund, turning down marriage proposals as it suits you. Your parents would not countenance it. They sent you here to learn the skills of a wife and a noblewoman and then to serve them well by marrying. To talk as if anything else were possible is nonsense."

"Is it impossible to marry with some degree of affection?" cried Rosamund, suddenly uncaring of her manner when she had so little to lose by it. "Would it be so terrible that I might chance to even like someone before I were instructed to marry them?" Tears sprang suddenly to her eyes, something that had never happened so commonly to her as in the past weeks. At Rosamund's renewed tears, Iolanthe sighed loudly, but not entirely unsympathetically.

"I understand your feelings, my dear," she said in a kinder tone. "But if you ever imagined that you would marry for love, then you have been fooling yourself, and it is on that account that you feel such unhappiness now. We cannot choose, Rosamund. It is not our position in life."

She moved toward Rosamund and patted her shoulder affectionately.

"It is not so bad, my child. I was your age once, allied to be married to someone I had only met once before in my life when we were both but children. It has turned out most satisfactorily. If he is a decent enough man at heart, you grow to a kind of love in time. It suits well enough. And Edward is not a bad man, though I concede his manners leave a little to be desired. You could be matched with worse."

Iolanthe's words were of no comfort to Rosamund. Even if Edward were not so unappealing to her, to be married to any other man meant she was cut off forever from Alexander, from the man she now knew she loved heart and soul.

Rosamund's escort to Florham consisted of

Monckton men-at-arms, so there was, she realized, no chance of a final journey with Alexander as her protector.

Maud cried copious tears as she bid Rosamund farewell. Iolanthe and Lord Aelward were effusive in their regrets at letting her go but could not disguise their pleasure that a suitable match had been made for her so swiftly and now came to fruition.

Lord Robert, now back to full strength, also seemed genuinely sorry to see her go.

"I have greatly enjoyed our rides and our conversations, Lady Rosamund," he said with vigor. "And I shall not forget your efforts on my behalf when I was injured. I wish you every happiness in your new life."

Rosamund was touched. In contrast, Milicent gave Rosamund but a cool embrace in parting. Rosamund wondered if she intuited a look of satisfaction on Milicent's face as she stood to witness Rosamund's departure, but it mattered little to Rosamund now. She busied herself with good-byes to Alice and Godith and thence to servants, such as Brunhilde, who had also turned out to wish her well.

Alexander was not present to see her leave, and Rosamund noted his absence with pain. Yet she knew that to look upon him for the last time and keep her composure, in the presence of so many eyes, might have proved an impossible task. There would have been but a few stilted words of farewell possible between them, an exchange utterly inadequate to convey the depth of sadness she felt at their final parting. No, it was better that he had not come.

Rosamund was treated with every courtesy at Florham. Her room was to her liking; Lord Monckton and the baroness were cordial though lacking in the warmth of the Aelwards that had so struck Rosamund on her first acquaintance with them. Even Edward, whom she had been loath to meet again, seemed of civil temperament. But Rosamund still shuddered in trepidation at her fate.

She spent a sleepless first night in her new surroundings, and by dawn she knew her lack of repose must have affected her judgment, for she was resolved upon a course of action that had not an ounce of sense to commend it. She had to tell Alexander of her feelings. Her silence up until now seemed no longer an act of decorum but one of cowardice. If she were now committed to an unhappy marriage, then how could the revelation harm her more? If he were to find out, Alexander would almost undoubtedly do nothing save humor her politely and express his regret that he had stirred her to such unhappiness. On the evidence of previous occasions, the chances of him breaking her confidence seemed small, but even if he did so, Rosamund could hardly summon the self-preservation to care. The worst that could happen would be for Edward to hear of it and reject her, and even the fiercest disapproval from either the Aelwards or her parents on that score scarcely seemed a poorer outcome than marrying him.

But by noon, her almost feverish thoughts had been replaced by a deep depression. She had no means of communicating with Alexander. She could hardly ask Lord Monckton, on the strength of one day's acquaintance, for the services of a messenger to deliver a letter. Furthermore, even if she were able to send such a missive, secreted in a letter to Maud perhaps, there would be no time for Alexander to respond before her wedding, even if he chose to. For a very short time, Rosamund considered appropriating a horse from the stables and riding to Duloe herself, before the foolhardiness of such an action persuaded her otherwise. A full day's journey alone without provision contained too many dangers for even her desperation to overrule.

■ ■ ■ ■

As if drawn to a familiar comfort, Rosamund excused herself after the midday meal and made her way unobtrusively to the stables. The fight had faded in her. She no longer had any realistic notions of messengers or solitary horseback rides, but to be in the proximity of the stables' equine residents reminded her, in her hollow sadness, of the only times she had ever exercised any measure of mastery over her own fate: the times when she rode out alone on her father's estate, free to choose her own path and answerable to no one.

She had no idea if Edward Monckton would even allow her to ride.

Filled with a rush of anger again at the new fetters that would now fall upon her at the whim of her husband, she picked up her skirts with purpose and decided to leave the confines of the stable courtyard. She might well be chastised for walking alone, but she did not have it in her to care.

The breeze of the late summer afternoon calmed her senses a little, and the fading green of the meadows on either side of the track she followed formed a pleasing vista heedless of her melancholy. The manor house was soon out of sight as the track dipped into a vale. Rosamund had walked for but a short time when she was distracted from her thoughts by the sound of an approaching rider. She stopped, entertaining a momentary uncertainty. The visitor would most likely feel obliged to stop and greet her and would almost certainly mention her solitary presence when he arrived at the manor house. Well, Rosamund thought reluctantly, it would provide a measure of the Moncktons' character as to how they responded to news of their wandering soon-to-be daughter-by-law.

Preparing to address the stranger as he neared, Rosamund suddenly found her throat constricted. Her heart pounded in hope and disbelief, and a weakness nearly brought her to her knees. The rider was no stranger. There in front of her was Alexander.

She could not drop her gaze but looked up at his beautiful face, drinking in the sight of him. As he dismounted and walked toward her, the look on his face told her everything she could wish to know. His eyes did not break from hers as he drew closer. There could be no other reason for his presence. He is here for me, Rosamund cried out inside. Her own emotions must have been written upon her face, for it was with barely a pause as they reached one another before they were in each other's arms.

"But why did you come?" Rosamund asked tremulously when he finally released her long enough to speak.

"Do you need me to answer that?" he smiled gently at her.

She shook her head in confusion. "What I meant was, how did you know to come?"

"You have a good friend in Lady Maud," Alexander twinkled.

Of course, thought Rosamund, a smile of gratitude crossing her face. Brave Maud, for it could not have been an easy encounter to arrange.

"I have been a fool, Rosamund," said Alexander. "Quite the biggest fool."

Rosamund shook her head in mute disagreement. His one foolishness could surely only be to stand here with her now.

"No, it is true," he insisted. "I committed myself these last weeks to an engagement with Sabeline Henry in which my heart had no part, and I beg you to believe that. I forged the alliance only with thoughts of my duty to my manor. I wonder that you can find it in you to forgive me."

Rosamund found it easy to attribute such honorable motives to him.

"It is a dutiful reason to form an alliance," she insisted. "I know you have the greatest fondness for Wickford and its inhabitants." Then her face grew serious. "My own rank is much inferior to Sabeline's. It offers you nothing in the way of political alliance."

Alexander paused to brush away the soft tendrils of her hair that blew in front of her face.

"An advantageous marital alliance may be a duty, but it seemed too hollow a duty to me when I thought to undertake it with a woman I do not love." His own face grew sober at this. "And more hollow yet when I thought to pursue it at the cost of abandoning a woman whom I do love."

His words and his touch sent a rush of joy through Rosamund.

"Nay, it was a mistake," Alexander continued. "Yet even as I debated it after my brother's death, I might have counseled myself against it had I not heard of your own engagement. And had Lady Milicent not convinced me that you harbored an affection for Edward Monckton. It was a bitter blow to me."

"You thought I cared for him?" asked Rosamund in dismay.

"Aye, Lady Milicent was convinced of it," replied Alexander. "And once again, I was a fool for believing it instead of trusting my own judgment on your feelings toward him. It was only when Lady Maud spoke with me that it became clear I had been misled, though for what purpose I still know not."

"Milicent misled you gravely indeed," said Rosamund, in consternation at hearing of Milicent's pronouncement. She shook her head. "She has never liked my affinity with Lord Robert, and she and Sabeline formed a good friendship this summer. Mayhap she wished to help her friend secure what she desired." She scowled but then her face cleared. "I would be angry with her for meddling in such a way, but I cannot care too much. Not now you are here."

"Aye, let us forget her now," agreed Alexander. "She has not had her way in this and is considerably displeased over it. But I owed a considerable apology to Lady Sabeline, no matter the circumstances of our engagement."

Rosamund absorbed the words Alexander had just spoken. "Milicent is already displeased?"

"I have already broken my engagement off," Alexander confirmed. "Almost as soon as you had left and Maud had spoken to me, I determined what action to take. I wrote to the Henrys immediately, and I set off for here as soon as I could. I did not wish to arrive too late."

So he had broken off his engagement even before he came to find her. Rosamund's heart swelled even more.

"But let me first tell you," Alexander said, "that even without Maud's blessed tale, which was music to my ears, I should have long ago persuaded myself that you could not have kissed me as you did in the forest if you had not had some feeling for me. Tell me I am right," he insisted.

Rosamund nodded her head, tears welling.

"Then I imagined how I would feel to see you married, and I having never taken the trouble to find out how you truly felt about me.

"For a short and foolish time after I heard the news of your betrothal I thought that it was for the best. I took pitiful comfort in the ideal of courtly love between a knight and a lady who is married. I thought I could worship you from afar and it would take nothing from my ardor for my duties, nor from my own intended marriage of convenience." He paused to give a bitter laugh. "But then I realized almost instantly what a mad fool I was to think as much. I confess I could not stand the thought of that over-bearing buffoon marrying you. And what of you? Your unhappiness in this would make a mockery of my chivalric vows. How could I take honor in discharging my duties else-where when I had left you in the hands of such a man? No," he shook his head. "The mist cleared from my mind. I knew I could not stand by and watch this happen. I have already lost one person I love this year. I cannot lose another."

He stroked her cheek with his thumb. "You are crying."

With a fierce hand, Rosamund wiped away the tears that had sprung unbidden.

"I prayed you would come," she confessed. "Even though I thought it nothing but a foolish fantasy. Ever since I arrived here, I have been taken up with regret that I said nothing to you of my feelings before I left. I have been thinking of ways to reach you, to tell you . . . to tell you . . ." She faltered at the step that she was about to take. "To tell you that I love you. Before it was too late and you yourself were married."

Alexander was silent for a moment as he held her. Then he spoke.

"You have made me happier than I can say with your words." He looked deeply at her and she felt dizzy with the nearness and intensity of him. Then with his mouth softening, he asked, "Had you no wit at all as to my feelings for you?"

Rosamund shook her head. How far back could she start in an account of the heartache she had suffered over him in the last months?

"But I asked you for a token at the tournament. And none other."

She smiled faintly. "I feared that you asked merely out of etiquette. Everyone talked of you and Sabeline as a match."

His expression was one of amused exasperation and then chagrin. "Well, I cannot blame you for thinking that. After all, it is what came to pass for a very short while. Lady Henry can be very persuasive to a man who believes he has missed his chance to marry for love.

"Nay," he continued. "It is you I have wanted from the very first. Perhaps even since you showed your spirit in the forest at your father's home. Certainly the more I saw of you at Duloe." His eyes darkened. "And I knew I loved you when I saw you tending those soldiers after battle. I knew it when I kissed you in the forest, though I feared you thought ill of me for doing so."

"I did think ill of you for a short time,"

confessed Rosamund. "But only because you spoke not of it, and I thought you must not care for me. Then when you apologized I thought it was because you regretted it."

"Such a fool am I." Alexander pressed the heel of his hand to his head. "Then I insulted you at both turns. I only regretted saying nothing at the time, and belatedly wished to reassure you that I was aware of my poor behavior, and that you deserved better than for someone to take advantage of you so."

"You did not take advantage," Rosamund admitted, a blush staining her cheeks as she spoke. A smile came to Alexander's face.

"Then I probably insult you more to suggest that you could be so easily swayed to an embrace against your will, for you are a woman who knows her own mind."

"It was for that reason I could say nothing of my feelings," said Rosamund. "For fear you would think badly of me, a woman desiring the kiss of a man she has no connection to."

Alexander put a gentle hand under her chin and tilted her face up, just as he had at the tournament.

"I could never, ever think badly of you for returning the feelings I hold for you." He was still smiling as he bent his head to hers again. When he released her again he said:

"This time in a fortnight we will be married. What say you?"

At these words Rosamund's heart could have burst with happiness. They stood smiling at one another in a gentle embrace, her fingers straying to his face and hair to caress him as though she could barely believe he were real unless she could feel him.

After a moment or two he asked: "Well? Do you have an answer for me?"

"An answer?"

Her face clearly showed her confusion, for he added: "Do you consent to marry me?"

Rosamund thought she might cry again. "Yes, yes," she whispered. "I will marry you. I can think of no greater honor."

"I can," he replied, drawing her to him so his chin rested in her hair. "And that is the honor of being your husband."

Letting her go for a moment, he slid his seal ring from his smallest finger on his left hand. "No one but a Ringewar wears this ring, and all who see it know it. It is yours, from today until we wed. My promise to you." He pressed it into Rosamund's palm. Still unbelieving in her happiness, Rosamund reached down with her other hand to touch it.

"And now," he continued, "Now we have

some matters to attend to. I will explain all at Florham. Then let us return to Duloe and announce our intentions."

Alexander was true to his word. Two weeks to the day, as the sun was at its highest in the sky, Rosamund stood at the altar in the chapel at Wickford, dressed in wedding robes of silk and lace as light as thistledown, her knight by her side as they spoke the vows their hearts had already made to one another so many months ago.

The employees of Thorndike Press hope you have enjoyed this Large Print book. All our Thorndike, Wheeler, and Kennebec Large Print titles are designed for easy reading, and all our books are made to last. Other Thorndike Press Large Print books are available at your library, through selected bookstores, or directly from us.

For information about titles, please call:
(800) 223-1244

or visit our Web site at:
http://gale.cengage.com/thorndike

To share your comments, please write:
Publisher
Thorndike Press
10 Water St., Suite 310
Waterville, ME 04901